"Wait till ...
turning her toward the mirror."

At the sight of two muddy hand prints decorating the front of her cotton dress, Darcy groaned. "Oh, no. This looks as though…"

"It does, doesn't it?" he said, grinning.

"It's not funny," she complained, stepping away and facing him. "You shouldn't be pawing women you don't even know."

He put on a serious face. "Oh, come on, Darcy, it's not as though I don't know you. Here, let's see if we can dust you off." Before she could protest, he flicked his hand across her chest in a rough flurry, raising hot thoughts.

In danger of melting, she reached up and grabbed his hand. "Maybe I should go home and change," she said. Her palm burned from his thumb and she dropped his hand, silently cursing her hormones. The air crackled with tension.

He looked at his hand, glanced at her chest and pursed his lips slowly. She had the crazy notion that she knew exactly what he was thinking. He was thinking about kissing her breasts.

She was breathing fast, audibly, but she couldn't help it. She had an even crazier notion to arch her back and lead his mouth where it wished to go.

Dear Reader,

My introduction to romance novels came when I was assigned by a major newspaper to write about two successful romance writers—Shirley Larson and Helen Mittermeyer. Their work intrigued me. In the world of romance, life could take an unexpected upturn, or old dreams could be rekindled, new dreams made. This is what *The Better Man* is all about. I hope you enjoy it as much as I loved writing it!

Though I consider Washington, D.C. my adopted home, my husband and I currently live in the rolling countryside of Upstate New York with five horses, cats, geese and visiting wildlife. I love to hear from readers, so please write to me c/o Harlequin Temptation, 225 Duncan Mill Road, Don Mills, Ontario, Canada, M3B 3K9.

Sabrina Johnson

THE BETTER MAN
Sabrina Johnson

Harlequin Books

TORONTO • NEW YORK • LONDON
AMSTERDAM • PARIS • SYDNEY • HAMBURG
STOCKHOLM • ATHENS • TOKYO • MILAN
MADRID • WARSAW • BUDAPEST • AUCKLAND

To my own hero—my husband.
And to my family for encouraging me to write fiction.

ISBN 0-373-25719-8

THE BETTER MAN

Prologue

THE ROSES in Darcy Blair's bouquet wilted as miserably as she did, waiting for George. She feared something awful had happened to the man she loved. It wasn't like him to be late for a date, much less for his own wedding. The small stark anteroom of the church in Washington, D.C., was hot, but she was shivering.

Her eyes softened as she thought of how big blond George Templeton, her husband-to-be, loved to tease and shock her. She expected him to do something dramatic; maybe he'd arrive in a helicopter.

After another half hour of waiting, her head throbbed with images of poor George lying crumpled and bleeding in a ditch. Even when her friends called the hospitals and found he wasn't there, she was sure something terrible had happened.

The beautiful lace neckline of her wedding gown scratched her collarbone, and her shoulders slumped under the heavy satin. Loosening a button at her throat, Darcy tried to tune out the whining of the organ music. She set the bouquet of roses down on a small table. Its overly sweet smell was only adding to her headache.

She glanced around the room. Six of her friends stood in a silent crush of peach satin, having voiced every plausible excuse and platitude—summer traffic in the nation's capital was horrendous, George had an awful hangover, he'd gone to the wrong church, his tux was getting altered.

Darcy loved them for not voicing her other sickening fear—George was dumping her publicly. Maybe he'd realized his mistake in proposing to a woman who could never fit into his life in the fast lane—the daughter of a waitress. He'd said it didn't matter, that he loved her because she was introverted and shy.

"You're my anchor. My beautiful anchor," he'd said, and remembering his sincere face, she pooh-poohed the idea that he'd just chosen not to appear. Her nervousness had conjured up that thought, nothing more.

In the far corner Josh, the best man, leaned against a wall. He was obviously angry. A patch of sunshine created highlights in his dark hair and flickered across the hard planes of his face.

Josh's anger surprised Darcy. She didn't think he'd approved of his friend marrying a waitress's daughter. In fact, she'd had a nagging suspicion that Josh knew George's *exact* whereabouts.

She walked over to him and said, "Well, Josh, where do you think George is?"

A vein throbbed in Josh's temple and he stared straight ahead. Darcy bit her lip. She wished Josh would share his opinion on what was happening, but he didn't and she didn't know him well enough to push. And, of course, George could walk in any second with an honest excuse. She glanced toward her parents.

Her mother's blond hair, so much like her own, was getting frizzy in the humidity, lifting in a cloud that hovered over her frown. Her father paced the room, red-faced, fists clenched, trying hard to contain his temper, she knew.

Hearing a tentative knock on the door shot hope through her, but when she whirled around she saw Josh in the doorway, dark head bowed, holding a slip of paper. She ran up and grabbed it, crying, "What's happened? Is George okay?"

In answer, Josh handed her the paper. It read, "Tell her it's off." Darcy's horrified gasp filled the room. Her father rushed up and she steadied herself against the door, as he read the note aloud, voice trembling.

Her dad's face turned purple, and his eye twitched. "I'll shoot the bastard!" he cried, twisting around toward the door.

Her mother, blinking through her tears, grabbed her husband's arm. "Ralph! You've got to calm down."

"Calm down?" he shouted. "The bastard's disgraced us. I knew he thought he was too good for us."

But her mother clung to his arm firmly. "Darcy needs you now. Our daughter is too good for him. Let it be. We'll get through this."

Her dad reached for Darcy and pulled her close, anchoring her to his broad chest. His lapel rubbed softly against her cheek, absorbing her tears. Her mother, Cora, put an arm around Darcy, too, surrounding her with unconditional love.

"I have to inform the guests that they can all go home," Ralph said, releasing Darcy.

Cora grabbed his arm. "Why waste all the food? Let's tell the people to go to the hotel and eat."

Reluctantly her dad nodded, and as he shuffled off, Darcy lowered her head into her hands. Her parents had been too proud to let George's folks pay for the wedding; they'd dipped deep into their savings to put on a lavish spread for their only child. And Darcy's friends had worked since dawn to cook up an elegant feast of roast beef, turkey and shrimp, as well as scrumptious hors d'ouvres carefully arranged on silver trays.

Darcy tried to tell her shattered self not to cry anymore, but through her tears she saw Josh approaching and she cringed. His lips moved, but no words came out. He reached for her hand and held it tight. She bristled, certain that Josh was about to make some excuse for George.

Drawing a deep breath, he said, "Darcy, look. This is a terrible thing to have happened. I'm so sorry."

She felt his arm slip around her and she stood furiously blinking back the tide that lapped at her eyelids. She didn't want pity from George's best friend and messenger. As she tried to pull away, he leaned down and kissed her on the forehead. "Wait, Darcy," he said, "I'll call you."

Pulling away from him, Darcy stood seething. Call her for what? To say she was stupid? To tell her she really shouldn't have aspired to marry a Templeton?

As for his little kiss, it was totally out of line. It wasn't as though Josh was her friend. Hadn't George told her Josh was a lady-killer? It figured he'd actually think she was easy pickings, prime for a quick roll in the hay. She swept past him and went to thank her bridesmaids.

ALONE AT LAST, Darcy searched her soul for clues, rehashing things she'd said that might have driven George to shove her into an emotional chasm the size of the Grand Canyon. And as she sorted through all her inner tumult, one painful word kept popping up in her head like a piece of burned toast. *Fool.* She was the biggest fool in the world. She'd fallen in love with a man who said he loved her but didn't. He'd betrayed her love and trust in front of everyone. He'd shattered her like a piece of cheap china.

She was never going to forgive George. And she would never fall in love with a rich man again. She would bury herself in work.

1

"I'M HERE to see the dream maker," the man outside her office said. "Is Ms. Blair in?"

Through her glass office door, Darcy could see his tall blurred shape and for a split second imagined she knew him. Perplexed, she swiveled around in her chair and grabbed her calendar. Maybe Amy, her receptionist, had penciled somebody in. But no. The day stood blank. She smiled. *Come on in and let your dream roll.*

Even if she'd had back-to-back appointments, though, she would have fit him in. He could be just the angel Dreams, Inc., needed to make her own dream a reality.

She quickly straightened the papers on her desk. Making her company a success had consumed Darcy's every minute for the past two years and her hard work had paid off. Dreams, Inc. had grown from catering small functions to planning fantasy weddings. A few more clients, one or two pricey show-biz weddings, and then her parents and Aunt June could buy back her grandfather's hardware store in Phoenix.

After finger-combing her bangs, she pressed the button on the intercom and told Amy to please send the visitor in. When her office door flew open, her mouth did likewise. Josh Cartwright stood there grinning, tall and confident in his expensive dark-striped suit. His brown eyes sparkled across her as though he had just won the state lottery.

Darcy gulped. The calendar she held fell from her hands. Her stomach knotted. "Hello," she managed to splutter. Twenty-four months had crawled by since he'd handed her that cruel note from George, but fresh humiliation and anger swept through her as the scene replayed itself in her mind.

"Darcy, you look fabulous," he said, gazing down at her as though he was her long-lost lover. "It's good to see you."

She barely avoided knocking over the vase full of fresh spring flowers that sat on her desk. She straightened the blooms with a trembling hand. She had seen Josh Cartwright whispering to George the first time he'd met her. And later George had told her Josh thought people should stick to their own side of the track when it came to marriage. Apparently George had listened to him in the end. She frowned. Josh was not her angel.

He planted himself in a chair, stretching his long legs. "Well, how have you been, Darcy?"

"Great. Just great. What brings you here?" She self-consciously pulled at her old beige suit skirt that was pulled unforgivingly around her waist. His superbly fitted suit and highly polished shoes cost more than her second-hand office furnishings.

"I saw this article yesterday and suddenly knew where you were hiding out," he said, and chuckled.

His laughter grated in her ears. She avoided George's friends, but she wasn't exactly hiding out. Her work took her to many public places. And she'd even dated several different guys. Nothing serious. She enjoyed going out to dinner and dancing.

"My hideout is very carefully designed, Josh—a room, padded with mattresses from floor to ceiling." She was shocked by her own words. For months after her disastrous wedding day, she'd fallen asleep imagining just such a protective cocoon.

"I like the mattress idea," he said. "It has unlimited possibilities for...fun. From floor to ceiling." He rested his eyes on her mouth.

She bit her lip. She hadn't told a soul about her cocoon, and it irritated her that she had told *him*, of all people. And he had trivialized what she'd clung to for months with a sexual innuendo that embarrassed her.

"What brings you here?" She stared at him as though he had crept out from under a rock.

He glanced away, looking hurt. "I'm here to discuss my sister's wedding," he said. "An article I read says you've become a successful wedding planner. The Viking wedding sounds particularly interesting—everybody in heavy armor, sailing around, uh, clunking around a cove. I don't know about the Bora Bora affair, though, with the bridal party in war paint and all the guests in grass skirts. Glad I wasn't invited to that one."

She silently cursed the article. "Only some of the guests, the good sports, wore war paint and grass skirts." *Bridal Ideas* magazine mocked her from her desktop. "Dream Maker Darcy Blair." In smaller print below: "She can make your dream wedding a reality."

He picked up the magazine and read those words that would never cease to embarrass her. "I'm surprised you've become a wedding planner," he said.

She felt her cheeks flame. She didn't need his pity. And she didn't need the implication that poor jilted Darcy couldn't leave the altar, even if it meant being there vicariously. She'd overheard that one nasty former friend had actually said that to somebody at a wedding she'd catered last week. At the time she'd felt helpless. Now it angered her.

"It's a lot more positive than working as a divorce attorney, don't you think?" she bristled.

"Divorce law, sadly, is big business," he replied. "My firm's business has doubled in the past two years. But that's not the only reason some of us are in it. For me, it's a way of helping people, as well."

She wasn't about to get defensive, too, and start explaining why she'd become a wedding planner. In fact, it had come about accidentally. A friend's plans had fallen apart and she'd been asked to step in to get forty hot-air balloons, holding bridal party and guests, launched across the Potomac.

He went on, "Of course, handling so many divorces should have jaded me, but I still think happy marriages exist. So, I'd like you to work on my sister's wedding. It's a big project, but I think you can handle it. And, anyway, how much work does planning a wedding take?"

"The article didn't convince you?"

"The article convinced me I should come and see you again." He smiled. "Working together is going to be fun."

She pressed her fingers to her temples. Despite the annoyance it caused, the magazine article had brought the hope of attracting new business. Not in a million years had she expected Josh Cartwright to come waltzing in.

"The story doesn't say whether or not you're married now. You're not wearing a ring, so I take it you're still on the loose?"

"I'm going to be on the loose, as you call it, permanently." She winced. What was the matter with her? She'd told him two deeply personal things—the cocoon and her vow. "Now, regarding your sister's wedding, I'm not sure we can handle it." The truth was she'd rather do just about anything else than have any dealings with Josh Cartwright.

"What's the problem?" he persisted, drumming his fingers on the arm of his chair.

"Depends," she hedged. "On when it is and what else is going on here. We may not have the time or the staff."

"You can always hire the necessary staff."

"We don't hire and fire people per wedding. We like to train people and hang on to them. We have four staffers." She paused. "Why are you here and not your sister?"

"She couldn't take time off from work today. We'd like to come back next week and discuss the details. Or better yet, you could have dinner with us."

Darcy hated the intimate way he gazed at her. As if offering to soothe away everything his best friend had done to her. *Opportunist.* Josh hadn't quit trying. She picked up her calendar from the floor, then pulled out one of the standard Dreams, Inc. forms.

"You need to fill this out." She thrust the long form across the table at him. "I'm not sure what next week is going to look like. We conduct our business during office hours, so dinner is out."

"I'll call your assistant for an appointment," Josh said. "And I take it you've developed the habit of returning calls?"

"I always return *business* calls, Josh." Why would he drag up the ancient fact that she hadn't returned his calls?

"And you can always tell why someone's calling?"

"Yes." As his gaze locked with hers, her heart fluttered. She disengaged the connection and focused past his shoulder at the small watercolor of her grandfather's hardware store.

He turned his attention to the form, reading it with the painstaking care of an attorney, while Darcy sat thinking of nature's excesses. Josh Cartwright was more handsome than she remembered. The unruly little waves in his brown hair demanded smoothing back into place. She rubbed her fingers together. Then she set her hand on her desk. Given Josh's reputation as a lady killer, womanizer, playboy, ladies' man, runaround, no doubt those waves got plenty of handling. Years of caressing fingers had probably created the waves in the first place!

She had news for Josh. Handsome and rich didn't impress her. People like him lacked values. She watched him filling out the form, and she leaned back in her chair, away from him, focusing on the pink blossoms of an almond tree outside the window, trying to fill her mind with happy pictures.

Josh wrote out a check and slid it, along with the form, across the desk toward her. "I'm sorry I've left a few blanks. Ginger will complete this next week."

Darcy took the form and studied it. "But you've left most of this blank," she said, then glanced at the check and gasped. She knew he was rich. Everybody in town knew about Cartwright Industries, makers of hi-tech medical products. He didn't have to flaunt it and sit there looking amused.

"Look," she said. "We require only a $100 deposit to begin with. Then we work in increments. So your $10,000 check is unnecessary." She pushed the check toward him. "In fact, since this form isn't really complete, why don't we wait till next week when your sister can fill this out? You can give me the check for the correct amount then—if this goes forward."

"I prefer to handle it this way for my own personal accounting reasons." He picked up her aqua-colored glass paperweight and set it on top of the check so firmly the little glass fish locked in the dome swam madly.

"You do understand we only organize lavish dream weddings?" she said. He had left the question on the form for the wedding theme unanswered.

"Yes." He smiled. "I'll let my sister fill you in. Ginger's picked a pretty weird theme for her big day."

He stood up. For the first time she noticed the size of her office. Small. Cramped. She rose and the top of her head barely reached his shoulders.

"Great seeing you again, Darcy, and I'm looking forward to seeing more of you."

His solicitous gaze, the way he spoke the words, with a heartfelt sincerity, told her he meant more than a mere cordial exchange between acquaintances. Disconcertingly she felt a soft feminine feeling wash through her.

He leaned across the narrow desk and kissed her on the cheek. A brief warm sensuous touch that teased her skin unbearably. Then he gave her a dazzling smile so full of pleasure her heart pounded and, deep within her, something snapped.

He strode out.

She sank down in her chair, fuming. He had no right to kiss her. His ego was bigger than any Washington monument, but she would cut it down to size. She swiveled around in her chair to the computer and began pounding out a formal note, informing Josh Cartwright that Dreams, Inc., could not fit his sister's wedding into their hectic schedule. She would mail his check along with the letter; get rid of him no matter how badly they needed his account.

JOSH'S BODY ACHED for her as he drove his red Jeep slowly out of the parking lot behind the small Dreams, Inc., building in Georgetown. It had been damn hard sitting across from Darcy, with the beautiful round face and eyes as blue as Lake Tahoe in the evening. Her lovely taffy-colored hair was fluffier than it used to be, with waves over her ears. And he liked the small sparkling earrings.

He wanted her—just as he had the first time he'd met her. It was at a party. He'd gone up to George and whispered, "This woman is different. Warm and genuine." And George had hissed back, "Keep away from her. I found her." Oh, he'd acted gentlemanly and backed off. A collosal mistake.

A honking horn snapped Josh out of his daze and prevented him from pulling out in front of another car. It wasn't like him to drive recklessly. But he was stifling an impulse to run back into Darcy's office and confess the wild idea that had gripped him when George hadn't shown up on their wedding day. He'd been tempted to ask her to marry him on the spot. The urge to do so had been almost overwhelming. Something wild and primitive. And seeing her today, that same urge had hurtled through him.

A few blocks away he parked his Jeep and strolled, smiling at strangers, thinking how beautiful Georgetown looked on a bright spring day, how green and bursting with new growth. He walked into Sans Souci restaurant and saw that Ginger had already arrived and claimed a table. He sat down, reached across the white linen tablecloth and squeezed his sister's hand.

Ginger beamed affectionately at him. "How did it go? Are you still keen as ever about Darcy? You're glowing, so you must be."

"Wait till you meet her. I'm glad you agreed to let me do this alone. She's really a genuine person, not at all like the others."

"You mean she isn't like the redhead who wanted a loan, or the pretty blonde who wanted you to invest in a computer cruise?" Ginger laughed.

The waiter arrived and recited the day's specials, after which they both ordered cheese omelets.

"Darcy didn't exactly go into orbit at seeing me," Josh confessed. "But I know that's because she's got me all tied in with George."

"Well, you *were* supposed to be his best man."

"That surprised me," he said. "We weren't exactly best friends. I liked going to his home, though. His family had these solid traditions, and his mother was great—always so kind and genuine. Like Darcy."

"I'm surprised you know so much about her."

The waiter brought their omelets, sprinkled with parsley and sided with fries. Josh drained his water glass before speaking again.

"The first time I met her, she stood out, and not just because she's beautiful. She did something very nice. One of the guests was sitting alone. A plain woman with bad skin, and it seemed like everybody was avoiding her. But Darcy went over and talked to her. Pretty soon she had the woman singing. And she could really sing, too."

"That *is* nice. It takes a woman who's comfortable with herself to reach out like that."

"Exactly. Some women only care about getting attention when guys are around. She was also kind to an old man, helped him up out of his chair. She did a lot of nice things."

Ginger smiled. "You do nice things, too, like sending flowers each month to the old women who enter the Community Kitchen recipe contest. It sounds like you and Darcy would make a good match. You know, with me getting married, I've been wondering when you're going to take the leap. Thirty is time."

Josh nodded. "Most people my age already have two kids and a mortgage. And you're right about Darcy. I wanted to take her out the first time I met her, but George told me to stay the hell away from her, so I did."

"You've always been loyal to a fault," his sister said, and for a moment they both ate in silence.

"When are we going to see Darcy to talk about my wedding?" Ginger asked at last.

"Next week. I'll let you know."

"It would be wonderful if you settled down, Josh. We could have a double wedding."

Josh chewed slowly. "I'm thinking about it, Ginger. I don't know how good I'd be at raising kids."

"You'd make a great daddy," Ginger said between bites.

"Think so? I didn't have role models, except for George's parents." Lately the desire to have his own family had been gnawing away at him. Four kids. That number had stayed constant in his mind ever since he was a kid. "If I have two sets of twins, my wife wouldn't have to go through four pregnancies," he mused aloud.

Ginger chuckled. "Then you'll be driving to twin conventions all year. They have a lot of those now."

He laughed. "Not likely, but I'll drive them across the country, from Niagara Falls to the Grand Canyon. Camping, fishing—family stuff that we never got to do."

Ginger polished off her last morsel of food and announced, "I'm planning on having a big family."

Josh lowered his head. "You're still young," he said carefully. They were having a pleasant conversation and he didn't want to ruin it by criticizing Billy again.

She loved the man, and maybe his suspicions about Billy Melrose being just another gold digger would turn out to be totally wrong. He hoped so as he gazed fondly at his sister. Marriage was such a big step.

As they left the restaurant, Ginger said, "Call me about next week. I can hardly wait to meet Darcy. Anybody my brother likes so much has to be great." She kissed him goodbye. "Thanks for lunch."

Josh drove to his office, got into one lengthy grueling meeting after another and went home exhausted.

He checked his messages. A redhead he'd taken to the opera last fall spoke breathlessly into his machine. "Josh, this is Lola. I'm having a party on Saturday night. Hope you can come." No. He didn't like those big parties anymore.

The investigator he'd hired to check out Billy Melrose spoke next. "I haven't turned up anything yet. He's either very clean or very careful."

Erasing the messages, Josh wished he hadn't had to hire a PI behind Ginger's back, but Billy was evasive—the man simply wouldn't talk. He drove an expensive Mercedes and lived in a big house in MacLean, yet all he had was a low-paying government job. Ginger was only twenty and she'd always counted on Josh to look out for her. He wasn't going to let her down, not like his own father had, first by leaving, then by returning her mail unopened, hanging up on her when she called. His father had done all that to him, too, and Josh knew how much it hurt.

He sorted his mail, changed into jeans and turned on the TV just as the phone rang. He switched off the TV and picked up.

It was Sam Goldman, a buddy and a confirmed bachelor who loved to go out and raise hell. Josh enjoyed his friendship.

"Listen, Josh," Sam said. "I told you about those two Indiana blondes who are looking to party. Why don't we go meet them at the Razor's Edge?"

Josh hesitated. Hell, he'd had it with going out and putting on a whole big macho act, guzzling beer, laughing loudly, asking and responding to the same old questions. Where are you from? Where do you work? And lately, none of the women he'd met were shrinking violets. They wanted to take and take before he even offered anything. And last month, when he'd politely pulled away from an aggressive woman, she had insulted his manhood.

"Sorry, Sam, I have other plans."

"You feeling all right, buddy? I've never known you to turn down a party."

"I don't like to party as much as everybody likes to think I do," Josh said.

Sam laughed. "Your plans must involve a hot chick you don't want me to meet. Okay, buddy."

After he hung up, Josh got himself a beer. Hot chick? Hell, Sam's reaction was no different from anybody else's. They all thought of Josh Cartwright as a womanizer, and it was his own damn fault. He'd gone along enhancing this false image by dating so many women.

If truth be known, though, he was lonely. Partying and running around hadn't made him happy. He needed a wife to share his pillow, his heart, his *life*. Darcy was the woman he wanted. Beautiful, sexy and warm, she would know how to create a family with solid values because he could tell she'd been raised that way.

He wanted to fill the old house in Virginia with kids and laughter. He wanted to build solid traditions with everybody eating together and making soup on cold days, planting a garden in the spring. Carrots and tomatoes and potatoes.

They would raise catfish or llamas. Something fun and ugly and challenging that he knew nothing about. But there was always room to learn. And to share.

He wanted Darcy. Having seen her again, he was sure of it, despite the cold reception she'd given him. He had to get to know her better, prove to himself that his instincts were right. But it seemed she was still in love with George, and it made him damn mad. He'd have to yank her into the very real present, with himself a big part of it. Hell, he couldn't wait till next week to see her. Tomorrow he'd call and move that damn meeting up.

2

DARCY LICKED the envelope addressed to Josh Cartwright. After pondering over it last night, the note she retyped now and enclosed read, "Dreams, Inc., unfortunately cannot accept new clients; we are booked solid for the next two years."

Guilt swept over her again. Turning down the Cartwright job rated right up there, second on the list of the stupidest things she'd ever done. But there was no way in hell she could deal with Josh. He brought a complication deeper than the messy past. He managed to remind her of that exciting phenomenon known as chemistry between a man and a woman, and he'd ruined her cocoon forever. Last night she couldn't get past wondering specifically what kind of endless possibilities he'd been alluding to when she'd revealed her secret. And she didn't even *like* the man. Nevertheless, she didn't look forward to explaining this turndown to Aunt June.

A happy babble came from the Dreams, Inc., kitchen as Darcy entered, and a delicious aroma of chives cooking in butter rose over the industrial stove. Rosa, the main cook, stood stirring together a mushroom stuffing for the National Women City Planners' luncheon they were catering that day. She and her two helpers called out fondly to Darcy, "Good morning!"

"Hi, gang," she said. "What can I do to help?"

"Don't you have a wedding to plan?" Aunt June smiled and winked. "I saw Josh Cartwright yesterday on his way out, and he said you were going to work on his sister's wedding. Then—"

"And what a handsome guy!" Rosa cut in. "I was walking by your office when he, uh, expressed an interest in you."

Darcy turned red. *He had no right to kiss me.* "He's an old friend," she mumbled. "Would you like me to make some radish roses?"

"Changing the subject, eh?" Rosa laughed. "It's okay. If I was young and beautiful, I'd go after that sexy guy myself." She pointed to a huge bowl of radishes and turnips. "Since you're the best garnisher we have, I can't turn your offer down." She handed Darcy a small paring knife.

Swiftly carving the radishes and turnips into roses and tossing them into ice-cold water, Darcy listened to the others talk about shopping and movies. Everybody got along so well. She felt even guiltier about turning down the biggest, most profitable wedding job they'd ever had, considering he had marked the budget question with, "Whatever it takes." She finished off the vegetable roses and set them in the refrigerator.

"Can we talk, Aunt June?" she asked quietly.

June followed her to her office, carrying a steaming cup of coffee. "I started to tell you, Darcy, I got in about eight this morning and Josh Cartwright was on the phone. He'd like to come in today with his sister. My, this is exciting."

Yesterday Aunt June had run in as soon as Josh left, to discuss the prospect, as she usually did, and Darcy had given her Josh's check because she didn't want it getting lost in her messy office. Darcy realized now she'd better be blunt. There was no easy way to say what she had to say.

"I can't do it. I just can't work with Josh. I can't have him walking back into my life. I've typed this letter, and if you'll please give me that check, I'll mail it to him now."

Her aunt's face paled. She fiddled with her pearls. "Why not, dear?"

"Because, well, you know what happened. You were there. He brought the note from his friend George, who then married . . ." Her voice cracked. She couldn't say Rhonda's name, Rhonda, the woman George had left her for. "And you know, Aunt June, I think I've built up my wedding-planning business well, but I can't handle ghosts."

"Wait a minute, Darcy. I understand your anger at George. I'm angry at him, too. But Josh didn't do anything to hurt you."

"He could have warned me. Josh is too conscious of social status and money. He knew what was going on. But he didn't act like a gentleman and warn me, did he?"

Aunt June stared at her nails. "I don't know how to say this without upsetting you more, dear, but I think this is a case of killing the messenger."

Darcy felt heat suffuse her face. She hated to argue with her aunt and couldn't bring herself to even discuss anything concerning that awful day. She had heaped dishonor on her family and had slaved at piecing her frazzled self back together. But yesterday had shown her how deep the hurt went when she couldn't ask Josh a single one of those questions she'd rehearsed asking, if she ever saw him face-to-face.

"Aunt June, please don't misunderstand. I do feel guilty. We only have three months before grandfather's hardware store goes up for sale again."

Aunt June set her coffee cup down, got up and paced the small office. "I wish my settlement would come through," she said.

Darcy's throat constricted. Aunt June's ex-husband had yet to come through with the bulk of the divorce settlement that her aunt counted on to buy back her father's store.

"They offered us the first option on the store after your dad. I went down there and met with those people, but you saw the letter their attorneys sent. The owner is getting old and, to him, it's just a business. He doesn't care if the new owners tear the place down."

"We can't let that happen. You and Dad promised your father you'd buy it back. Our family honor is involved. And memories. You know, as long as I remember, we talked about what fun you had in that store till the Great Depression came along."

Aunt June's eyes misted. "Dad never got over losing the place. He said if he had hung on to it, Mother would not have developed agoraphobia and eventually taken her life. He never understood he couldn't change things, that he had no choice but to come to Washington to look for government work."

"I know, I know. And he was lucky he found work on the resettlement road in Virginia." Darcy tossed the wilted bouquet of spring flowers into her wastebasket.

"Who would have thought Phoenix would become a boomtown with out-of-sight prices? It was nothing but a big patch of desert. But I loved it."

Darcy tapped a finger on her desk. There was much more at stake here than their heritage. Her dad's asthma had him wheezing and hacking every time he walked any distance at all. Torn, fighting off guilt, she clung to hope. "Look. Something else will come up. I hate to sound childish. At twenty-eight, I should be a mature woman, but I can't work with Josh."

"Think of this as a business, dear. We don't turn down clients because of their color or occupation or anything else. So why would we turn down someone because he reminds us of something we'd rather forget?" Aunt June drained her coffee cup.

Darcy groaned. Aunt June had a way of explaining things.

"Come on, Darcy. We need this big wedding. Beggars can't be choosers. Once you start working on it, you'll be fine."

After a long silence, thinking of her father working as a lumberyard manager forever, dreaming of fulfilling his promise to his father, Darcy said, "Well, I am a professional businesswoman and my family does comes first. We could have Amy work on this wedding. Or perhaps you could work with Josh," Darcy said, warming up to the idea. "There is absolutely no reason somebody else can't take care of this. I have to learn to delegate, so I may as well start now. Of course, I'll help from behind the scenes."

Amy buzzed her. "Mr. Cartwright on line two." Darcy picked up the phone, frowning.

"Darcy, it was good to see you the other day. I'm calling now to see if Ginger and I can meet with you today."

"Will you hold on for a second? June Blair, my aunt and partner, is here. Let me consult with her." She put Josh on hold and spoke desperately to her aunt. "Would you please tell him when you're available?"

Her aunt smiled and picked up the phone. "Josh, I'll be working with you, along with Amy. What time would you like to come in?"

Aunt June's face paled. Finally she said, "We are here to accommodate our clients, and if Darcy is the one you wish to work with, we will shift our duties around here for you. But Darcy is busy today."

Then, ignoring Darcy's frantic signals, Aunt June glanced over at Darcy's calendar and proceeded to set up an appointment for Josh. "She can see you tomorrow afternoon."

After she hung up, Aunt June turned to Darcy. "Thank you, dear, you won't regret doing the right thing for the family. Working with Josh won't be as tough as you think. He's very charming."

As soon as Aunt June left, Darcy bit into a chocolate bar and didn't stop till she'd finished it and licked her fingers. Then she rattled her drawers, looking for more candy she might have stashed. Not finding any, she thought how unfair life could be. Not for one single minute could she fathom working with that egotistical

arrogant Josh Cartwright. Oh, yes, for the sake of her
family, she would try, but she was damn sure one of
them would call it an untenable situation and end the
client relationship. And she was betting she could make
that happen.

DARCY SAID HELLO to Josh but wouldn't look at him after he bounced into her office the next day, all glossed
up in a dark suit, smile brimming triumph. It galled her
that he had refused to let anyone but her work on his
sister's wedding. Now Darcy hoped Josh's involvement did not extend beyond this preliminary meeting.
Men generally came in the first time or two, and then
mothers and grandmothers took over.

Josh sat down in the chair directly opposite her and
attempted small talk. "The weather is beautiful isn't it?
Wonderful spring."

"It's stormy," she replied curtly. "The rain blew all the
cherry blossoms off the trees."

"That was two weeks ago."

Of course she knew that. But she did miss the cherry
blossoms. They brightened up all of Washington.
However, the azaleas were beginning to bloom in
clumps and borders. And the dogwoods were sparkling white and pink against the blue sky.

The office door burst open. A perky little blonde in
a chic red suit walked in.

"I'm Ginger. Your assistant said to just come in." She
extended a hand with perfectly manicured long red
fingernails across the desk.

Darcy shook hands, then walked around the desk to
remove a pile of papers from a chair, making room for

Ginger. Josh's gaze on her made her wish she'd shed those extra seven pounds and gotten her hair trimmed. She had worn her navy blue suit, which made her feel efficient, not attractive. She turned and his eyes met hers with a direct male message that rushed heat to her face. She sighed, wishing she could toss off her professional pride like a pair of sunglasses and walk out. Instead, she motioned to Ginger to sit down. Her brother's ego wasn't the poor girl's fault.

Darcy returned to her own chair. She picked up a pen and tried to write, only to find she was using the wrong end of the pen. Hastily turning it around, she wrote, "Cartwright Wedding" on a sheet of paper.

Ginger leaned over, read "Cartwright Wedding" upside down and smiled proudly.

"I'm glad you've got Cartwright in there," she said.

"You're going to keep your name then?" Darcy asked, reminding herself that she'd have to make sure to get the names right on the bridal registry, napkins and favors and all the other paperwork connected with the upcoming wedding.

"Mother changed her name so many times, Josh thought it would be best if I hung on to one name," Ginger explained.

"Will your mother be working with you on your wedding?"

"Our mother died three years ago," Josh said.

"I'm sorry," Darcy murmured. Josh's prime role in this wedding planning made more sense now. His eyes flickered with sadness, and she found herself touched. "Ginger, do you have anyone else, an aunt or grandmother, you would like to participate in planning your wedding?"

"What's wrong with 'brother'?" Josh asked. "Or do you think only women can plan weddings?"

"Women are better at it." Darcy stared at her notes, partly to avoid his probing eyes. She knew he wanted her to approve his involvement, indicate she was pleased to see him. But she couldn't roll up the past that fast.

"Well, you'll have to put up with Ginger's brother," he said. Then he grinned.

He looks sexy when he grins. Why was that even entering her mind? She didn't care how sexy he looked. He enjoyed the distress he caused her in making her work with him, and it occurred to her now to change her stance. She smiled sweetly at him, then turned to his sister.

"When are you planning to get married, Ginger?"

"Six months and three days from today—October sixth." Ginger glowed. "And I'd like what I call a European wedding." She went on, "My mother was half Greek and half Italian and spent her childhood in Milan. So I'd like to include the things she liked from her childhood in my wedding theme."

"What a wonderful idea," Darcy exclaimed, genuinely excited. She had imagined the Cartwrights would think of something pretty but standard. A Victorian teaparty. A cruise down the Potomac. A *beaux arts* ball at the Corcoran Art Museum. She smiled. "This is a fun idea. Colorful. Exotic," she said.

Ginger's lips curved up in a quick little smile. Darcy glanced curiously at Josh, who sat frowning. He didn't show any enthusiasm for his sister's wedding, although Ginger didn't seem to notice.

The light played off the tumbling waves of his hair, and again she found herself distracted by his sexiness. She deliberately turned to Ginger.

"So tell me about your fiancé. How did you meet him?" She wished her voice didn't burst that way with nervous cheerfulness.

"Billy Melrose. He's tall and sandy-haired. We met on the bus, the D9 express that runs from northwest to downtown on the Whitehurst Freeway. It's only a ten-minute ride, so we fell in love fast." She laughed in the rehearsed way of people who've discovered they can tell a particular story and get a guaranteed laugh. It *was* cute and Darcy chuckled. Josh only rolled his eyes.

"My sister tends to exaggerate," he said. "She and Billy have known each other for six months now and they got engaged on her twentieth birthday last week."

"Well, I'm sure you wouldn't be planning to marry him if you didn't know him well," Darcy said, then winced. *I must stop traveling back in time.*

"Ginger knows Billy as well as anyone can," Josh said, scowling, "Billy likes his privacy, uh, a lot."

Darcy's head shot up. Josh made Billy sound like a mysterious fellow, ranging anywhere from a reclusive Howard Hughes to a con artist.

He caught her curious look, then held up a hand and said, "Let me explain our situation. In our case, we don't have a family tree. We have an orchard—a slew of stepfathers and stepmothers. And oddly enough, the only one still alive is my father's third wife, whom we've never met, and her two children. They moved to Melbourne, Australia.

"Our immediate family now consists of just Ginger and me. So I tend to be a little overprotective of this kid . . . I mean, young woman." He patted his sister's arm.

He was overprotective by nature, Darcy thought. It was one way to maintain control, position himself in the center of things. She smiled to herself. Josh, the take-charge guy. She could see him as a bossy child, pressing himself into any circle of attention Ginger drew.

"You're overprotective all right," Ginger said affectionately, patting her brother's arm in return. "Josh is like a mother hen. But he wants to throw us the best wedding."

It was easy to like Ginger. Open, bubbly, excited, she wanted to enjoy life and have everyone around her participate to the fullest. But Josh's face reddened.

"I can't talk her out of this one. This European thing is a little too much of a hodgepodge. We could think of a more American alternative, something connected with the Wild West, say, like a rodeo. Or white-water rafting or some other sports theme."

"Ginger, you have your heart set on this European theme, don't you?" Darcy asked gently, ignoring Josh's conservative protests. He didn't have to edit his sister's dream wedding.

"Yes." Ginger nodded and gave a giddy little laugh.

"The wedding your sister's talking about, Josh, is such a wonderful way of celebrating your mother's background. And living in Washington, I feel the worldwide connection, a sort of global sharing, and Ginger wants that, too, not some dusty rodeo."

He rolled his eyes again, and Darcy glanced curiously at Ginger. It wasn't her place to meddle, but a wedding planner frequently played referee, as she had in the Bora Bora wedding, where the bride's grandmother ran interference. Darcy asked Ginger several questions about her mother's favorite things, made quick notes and began to visualize the wedding.

"Oh, this'll be fun. Big airy tents with oriental rugs, silk pillows, brass trays," Darcy said. "You can have Greek music, Italian food, English roses, French wines and Swiss chocolates."

"It's a wedding, not a Broadway musical," Josh said.

Ginger groaned. "Josh has complained about my idea from the minute I mentioned it, and I think it has to do with it being such a mix of cultures."

"If I hadn't promised my mother on her deathbed that I would see Ginger married properly, I'd insist she elope," he said.

Darcy watched him sulk. The man lacked imagination and a sense of humor. He wasn't spontaneous and fun-loving like his friend George. A small pain stabbed through her.

"Well, where do you plan to hold the wedding?" Darcy asked. "Here in Washington?"

"Oh, no," he said. "Flint Hill, Virginia. That's about sixty-five miles west of D.C., you know, just near Shenandoah National Park. I inherited a farm out there. The Blue Ridge Mountains in the background will be our version of the Swiss Alps."

Darcy picked up a pen and added the information to the form he had left incomplete. She heard him say her name and she glanced up.

The tenderness in his gaze stirred her. "Darcy," he repeated, and something about the way he said it held her attention. She looked into his chocolate brown eyes and felt her pulse quicken.

"You have a nice way of getting your clients excited," he said.

The way he pronounced "excited," with his eyes echoing a magical pause, related directly to his hormones. And it brought a small furtive smile to her lips. She returned her attention to the form.

"We have to run now, Josh. I have to get back to work," Ginger said, rising. "It was great meeting you, Darcy. You're wonderful."

Darcy smiled. Ginger's presence definitely helped. Her wedding theme held adventure. She was fun.

"Darcy, would you have dinner with Billy, Josh and me tomorrow night so you can meet Billy and we can talk some more about our wedding?" Ginger asked.

Josh shot his sister a pleased grin. Darcy was relieved it wasn't his idea, but she had always drawn the line at social engagements with clients. Aunt June walked in then, as she always did when new clients were involved, and introduced herself, eager to meet Ginger.

Ginger said, "Look, Darcy. I can't get time off from work. And Billy can't, either. I would like you to meet him. Please."

"If you can't get time off from work, Darcy will be delighted to meet you for dinner, won't you, dear?"

Darcy scowled and resentment toward her aunt filled her until her gaze fell on the hardware-store painting on the wall and her father's coughing and wheezing. She remembered his asthma was getting worse, he needed to breath the dry Arizona air.

"Okay, we can have a business dinner," Darcy said pointedly for Josh's benefit. "I'll bring as much information as I can get on tents and whatever else I can find."

"Tomorrow then," he said, smiling and leaving his business card on her desk.

After they left, Aunt June twirled her pearls and smiled, as though a load had been lifted off her shoulders.

"I know you didn't want to do this, Darcy, but I'm proud of you for setting aside your own feelings," she said.

"Ginger wants a unique European wedding, so I'm pleased. And she's a nice young woman. No family left other than her brother. He's worried about the man Ginger is marrying."

"Oh, dear, I hope that doesn't mean a cancellation." Aunt June sighed. "We'd have to return this hefty deposit, and without Dreams, Inc., for collateral, we won't get the loan to buy back Dad's store."

The unspoken—her father's health—caused Darcy's heart to sink, but she had to find an alternative. "I'll just have to look for more work. Martin is going to a dentists' function tonight. He invited me, and I'll try to work the room, see what I can drum up." Darcy picked up Josh's business card and slid it into a red lacquered box. Out of sight.

Her aunt sat down beside her. "You know, I've been meaning to ask about Martin. How's it going?"

"Same as always. He's a nice guy, but we're just friends. I told you that. We both like antiques and going to garage sales." She paused. "Reminds me, I'd better make some calls."

Her aunt left. Darcy rubbed her cheek where Josh had kissed her last week. This time she had distanced herself from him, anticipating another ridiculous brush on her face, but he hadn't even tried. Why did this creep into her thoughts, anyway? She didn't care one way or the other.

She had work to do, and tonight, if she *did* drum up more business, she could still return his check and recommend he hire Perfect Weddings, the big new Dreams, Inc., competition. Just last week she had disagreed with Aunt June about mailing out copies of the *Bridal Ideas* article to a long list of prospects Dreams, Inc., had put together, because of her personal feelings connected with it. But now that the article had brought in Josh Cartwright, how much worse could it get?

She began printing out the labels from that list, gave Amy the article to copy and began anticipating the dentists' convention tonight. Somehow, she was going to find a way to drum Josh Cartwright out of her life.

DARCY TOOK the stack of business cards she'd collected from last night's convention out of her purse and dropped them in the red lacquered box. Josh Cartwright's business card caught her eye. He had jotted his home number on it, and she saw that he wrote numbers with flair, with the eights leaning long, like his thighs. And next to his number, he had drawn a happy face that amused her—till she realized he'd given it a hairdo like hers, straight bangs and waves over the ears. He would never make it as a cartoonist.

Aunt June and Amy came in, chattering about the lunch they had catered.

"The Women City Planners are a serious bunch," her aunt said, "but they loved the food. We got some great compliments, and one of them inquired about our wedding planning. Her daughter is a skier, and they're thinking of ski-slope nuptials. In Vail."

Darcy stood up and cheered.

"But they don't have a date yet, so she's going to get back to us," Aunt June said. "Of course, I'll follow up."

"Hey, a prospect is a prospect." Darcy smiled. She knew the disappointment that frequently accompanied prospects, but the hope they would sign on the dotted line always sent her spirits soaring.

"Tell us about the dental convention," the two clamored.

"Lots of capped teeth. Expensive clean smiles." Darcy laughed. "I brushed my teeth for ten minutes before Martin picked me up." Her colleagues chuckled. Then she held up the stack of business cards. "I handed out our cards every chance I got. And I really concentrated on the spouses, hoping *their* businesses would hire us."

Her aunt beamed. "Smart girl."

"But ineffective," Darcy groaned. "Not one taker. Lots of talk. Cocktail-party chatter. I was hoping somebody would want to have a dental wedding. Everybody strapped in. Novocaine, instead of champagne."

Amy burst out laughing. And Aunt June tweaked her niece's chin fondly.

"I've got to get to the library," Darcy said, gathering up her notebook and purse. "I want to research props."

She walked to the library three blocks away. Georgetown was bustling, and she had to dodge cyclists. Music filled the air, and as she approached the saxophonist playing on the street, Darcy stopped to join his clutch of admirers. Today he sounded melancholy, and she dropped a dollar into his hat. The wonderful smell of french fries beckoned from a nearby restaurant, but she moved on fast. This tendency to eat when things weren't going right depressed her.

Hearing people chattering in several different languages, Darcy played her guessing game. She could identify French, Greek and German but had no idea about the nasal-sounding language two men in suits were speaking. Serbian? She walked on.

Just fifteen minutes after she arrived at the Georgetown library, the air-conditioning died with a hiss. Darcy fanned herself with a magazine and continued researching various European wedding details. One book, titled *Greek Rituals*, turned out to be a graphic sex guide from ancient Greek times to modern day, illustrated with erotic photographs of men and women in acrobatic sexual positions.

She studied one picture of a naked brown-skinned handsome man, with hair as dark as Josh's reclining on a lounge in front of the Parthenon sucking on an olive. His mouth was curved the same way Josh's had when he spoke her name. She felt a surge of heat and she slammed the book shut.

She glanced through several other books, then selected three to take home. She retrieved *Greek Rituals* and flipped through it till she found the picture of the naked man and stared at it again, then quickly slid the book back on the holding desk. After checking the three books out, she walked back to Dreams, Inc. Amy stopped her by the water fountain.

"Josh Cartwright called," she said.

Darcy clutched the books. "What did he want?"

"Didn't say. I told him you were out and asked if there was a message, but he said no."

Darcy hoped he was canceling dinner. It would give her more time to network, call old acquaintances to remind them about Dreams, Inc. The upcoming sale of the hardware store in Phoenix worried her no end. If they didn't come up with the money in three months, the cartel would go forward. Well, a bird in the hand... She better start working on Ginger's wedding. Darcy began making her calls, working from a long list she'd prepared. After ordering round brass trays to serve as tables at the wedding, she turned her attention to renting camels. Ginger's and Josh's mother, an imaginative lady, had told her daughter, "Ginger, when you get married, your groom will come riding on a camel," and so camels were now included. Darcy made a few calls.

The local zoo refused. A Cincinnati Zoo spokesman referred her to a man in Maine. "He raises camels for Hollywood. Keeps them in his indoor horse ring," he said. It sounded bizarre enough to be true. The phone rang and rang, but no one picked up and Darcy went on down the list. Food.

Several Italian caterers were listed in the Yellow Pages. She dog-eared the pages for later use. Then she turned the pages back to check on Greek caterers, wondering how baklava and stuffed grape leaves would go with Italian food. She wasn't sure about Josh's tastes in food, except that he talked like a steak-and-potatoes man. She doubted he wanted his highfalutin guests served a mishmash of food.

Thinking of the upcoming dinner, Darcy smoothed down the skirt of her melon-colored dress. The fuller-cut top made her figure appear more balanced, but she knew she had to go on a diet. Soon. Immediately.

Amy popped in. "Lunch?"

Darcy paused, opened her mouth to refuse, then grabbed her purse and the two of them dashed down the street to try to beat the noon-hour crowd.

The closest sidewalk café, Marianne's, bustled with young career people, sitting under big green umbrellas between potted plants. The aroma of roast beef and onion soup filled the air, and Darcy grinned at Amy.

"Let's grab a table," she told her friend.

"Josh Cartwright is a handsome man. Single?" Amy asked when they sat down.

"Single and dating up a storm, from what I've heard."

"He seems to have a real thing for you. Like Rosa, I saw him kiss you on the cheek. Why don't you see where it goes?"

"Amy, I'm not interested in the likes of Josh Cartwright. Wealthy and selfish. I've seen that before."

"You can't paint everybody who's rich with the same brush. How will you know if you don't give him a chance?"

Darcy devoted her attention to the menu. She didn't need to give Josh a chance to know how poor she felt in the company of rich men, especially having found it out the hard way with George. Amy meant well and they were good friends, but Darcy didn't care to discuss Josh Cartwright this minute. Or ever.

"I hope your Women City Planners lead comes through, and we can do the ski wedding." Darcy changed the subject and rushed through lunch.

They returned to work. Her office needed tidying but the phone was ringing, and by the time she finished going methodically down her list, a good part of the afternoon had swept by. Remembering her promise to help Rosa, Darcy returned to the kitchen. Planning exotic parties like the Jamaican bash the company was catering, always filled her with happy pictures. Golden sun-soaked beaches. Squawking colorful parrots. Palm trees dropping coconuts. Darcy started slicing juicy golden mangoes and star fruit, dreaming of roaming the world someday. Had Josh traveled much?

She wrapped the glass bowl of sliced mangoes and set it in the refrigerator. Lost in thought about her work, she rushed to her office, only to come to a halt in the doorway. Josh was there.

Wearing a navy blue blazer and gray slacks, he was sitting in a chair looking like a serious student, poring over a fat black file folder. His dark lashes brushed his cheekbones, and his dark eyebrows knotted as he read on. Something stirred within her.

Then he looked up. His eyebrows unknotted and his eyes tangled so deliciously with hers Darcy ran her tongue across her lower lip. Watching her, he rubbed the tip of his finger across his lips. She drew in a breath and glanced away.

"I left my pen here yesterday and just stopped in to get it. Hope you don't mind," he said, rising, holding up a sleek expensive gold pen.

Josh didn't strike her as forgetful. "I don't remember seeing it," she said, glancing around the cluttered room.

He laughed. "It's hard to tell in here. Was there an earthquake I missed?"

She frowned, taking in the piles of papers and catalogs and stacks of kites left over from the kite-flying wedding reception three months ago. But he didn't have to point it out and make a joke of it. She managed a weak smile. "There's a method to this madness. Creative people find comfort in disorder," she said.

Stashing his files in his leather briefcase, he asked, "Well, shall we head off for dinner? I can drive."

"Give me a second," she said, pointedly picking up the papers on her desk and stacking them randomly, making a bigger mess. "I suppose you live in an organized world where everything is in place."

"You can come see for yourself anytime, Darcy."

He looked so serious she stopped, papers in hand, quietly trying to unravel his body language. He seemed tense. A bad day at the office? He'd lost a case? His current girlfriend hadn't smiled when he'd expected it?

Then he laughed a bit harshly and said, "I read some research about pack rats. They collect everything unimportant to them and throw away the most valuable things in life—such as people." His voice grated like a cornstalk against metal.

Flabbergasted, Darcy dropped a pile of papers on her desk. His bitter message had to apply to George and his jilting her. Or he could be speaking of his family, the orchard as he'd called it, full of stepparents. Whatever his reason, it distressed her that he'd tied his bitterness into her lack of neatness.

The phone rang and, picking it up, she propped herself on the edge of her desk.

"Oh, hi, Mother," she said with genuine pleasure in her voice. "I had a wonderful time last Saturday night. You always make Uncle Albert's birthday special. He looks young for eighty-four, doesn't he?"

Suddenly she felt a hand on her thigh, fingers burrowing heat, and she spun around. Josh held up a piece of lint and smiled. Darcy felt her face burning and her thigh shook alarmingly.

Promising her mother she'd call her back, Darcy set the phone down and said, "I'll drive myself and meet you there."

"Parking's always a problem at the Raven's Nest, so why don't you just let me drive, unless, of course, you have some strange little thing about driving yourself everywhere?"

A silly little challenge and not worth fighting over.

"You can play chauffeur," she said, pleased with her simple answer. "Ginger and Billy must be on their way there."

He nodded and led her to the parking lot, then opened the Jeep door for her. She got in, smelling the faint tang of after-shave. He must have splashed some on before he got out of the Jeep and the thought that he'd done that for her interested her, made her wish she'd splashed on a little perfume herself. Something soft and feminine and sexy.

"I couldn't help overhearing you talk to your mother," he said as they pulled onto the road. "How is she doing? And how's your dad? It must be nice to have such a close-knit family."

She tensed. The last time Josh had seen them was that horrible day when he had witnessed their anguish and her humiliation. Those nasty images rose mercilessly in her mind. She took a deep breath and began chattering. "Mother and Dad are fine. They're eager about moving to Arizona." She heard her voice shake as though she was talking with a mouthful of ice cubes. The possibility that her grandfather's hardware store would sell to someone else made her heart sink.

Telling Josh about it was a waste of time. With his resources he wouldn't understand their inability to buy it back. Anyway, why even think of telling the man something so personal?

He glanced over at her and said, "Don't get so upset about them moving. You can always visit them. Or are you thinking of moving, too?"

The level of interest in his question surprised her until she decided he was simply making conversation. She sighed. "Some days I'm ready for all of us to move to Arizona. But we'd hate to leave Great-Uncle Albert. He likes his nursing home here."

She noticed the sadness on Josh's face, the slumped shoulders, and wanted to say something relevant and soothing to acknowledge that he had no family left. But he was talking.

"Billy was going to pick Ginger up after work, and I wanted to fill you in on a few things first regarding Billy."

He drove on and she waited but he said nothing, frowning, ostensibly concentrating on the Wisconsin Avenue traffic. Georgetown was crowded as usual, filled with tourists and natives shopping in the boutiques and lining up to get into the popular restaurants and bars.

"We'll go down Q street to avoid the traffic on M," he said. "Everybody slows down to listen to that guy playing the saxophone. I like his music, but I'm not crazy about his influence on traffic. He creates a gridlock."

She shifted in her seat. She loved watching the motorists' contented faces as they rolled the windows down and listened to the music. He turned on cobblestoned oak-treed, Q Street and, practically a hundred yards in, he stepped on the brakes. The screeching noise and the lurching of the Jeep made her gasp and brace herself.

"Damn it!" Josh said. "I think I hit a cat. Oh, why don't people keep their pets locked up?"

Face Ashen, he vaulted from the Jeep, waving to the cars behind him to go past, although there wasn't much room. If an oncoming driver took his eyes off the road for a second, Josh could get hit. He was standing in the middle of the street, turning this way and that and bending over recklessly.

"Be careful," Darcy cried. "Don't you get hit."

She saw him disappear below the hood of the Jeep. Fearful he'd been hit, she jumped out to help, holding up a hand to stop an oncoming car.

3

"GET BACK IN," he yelled.

"I'm not going to," she yelled back, running up to the front, standing protectively over him. He crouched on the street, head bent against the right front bumper, straining to retrieve the cat. Not hearing it meow, Darcy prayed silently.

He straightened up, holding a small coal black dog that squirmed and whimpered.

"Some cat," she said.

The driver of one of the cars behind them jumped out and hollered, "Hey, buddy, I've got a senator sitting in the car waiting to get to the White House!"

Josh transferred the dog to Darcy's arms and turned to the driver. "Tell the senator the president's gone to Camp David. The senator should keep up with the news." Motioning for Darcy to climb into the Jeep, Josh said, "Hold the dog. I'm going to pull over."

The little dog was warm and smelled of wet fur. She had never owned a dog, didn't even like dogs, but she desperately hoped for this one's survival. Dusk was beginning to soak up the light, making it hard to see the dog's injuries in the interior of the Jeep.

Josh double-parked by a fire hydrant and reached for the dog, who squirmed. As he tried to pick him up, his hand grazed her breast. Heat rushed to her face.

Switching on the interior lights, he gave her red face a curious glance. "There's a flashlight in the glove compartment," he said. "It'll help." His voice sounded oddly thick and he looked straight ahead.

The dog began bouncing and clamoring. Feeling a big wet spot on her chest, she looked down. The material of her dress had an area of blood or mud or both. Alarmed, she reached for the flashlight. The dog's filthy coat was matted and curled in heavy rough spots, but he had no obvious abrasions. She lifted his one white paw.

"He doesn't look hurt," she said, brushing the mud off her chest. "I'm so glad."

Josh turned the dog around to inspect his hindquarters. "It hasn't rained all week, fella. The streets are dry, so how did you get so muddy?"

The dog yelped and licked Josh's face. Josh grinned.

"No collar," Darcy said. "I wonder if he belongs to someone in one of these houses."

"As best as I can tell and judging from your dress, there's no blood, just a lot of mud. Looks like he's come a long way," Josh said, voice again oddly thick. He glanced sideways and laid his hand out, palm up, beside her.

Her chest rose and fell rapidly. She wanted to touch his hand, rub his palm with hers. "Let's set him on the street and see if he limps," she said, and seeing Josh nod, she climbed out with the dog.

Josh walked around the front of the car to where she'd set the animal on the cobblestoned sidewalk. They stood, heads cocked, observing the dog walking back and forth between them. He seemed weary but unhurt—and not at all anxious to leave his two new friends.

They knocked on doors and questioned anyone who walked by, but had no luck. Darcy, wishing she hadn't worn heels, leaned against the Jeep, rubbing one tired foot against another. The poor dog lay curled up on the seat in the car, and she could hear it whimpering through the lowered car window as Josh, tie loose and blazer slung over his shoulder, persistently questioned pedestrians.

She kicked off her right shoe, which had been mercilessly pinching her toes, and felt immediate relief.

"We should call the Humane Society," she said.

"I have a car phone, but I live just around the corner, so why don't we go there and make the call? There are a few animal-rescue outfits, so we'll call them all. Maybe we can get the dog situated."

She nodded and got back in, holding her shoe. Then she put the grubby little dog in her lap and cuddled him; his small size made him manageable. If he had been one of those big dogs, panting with his mouth open, huge wet tongue hanging out, she would have insisted he stay in the back seat.

"I'll call Ginger and Billy and tell them to come to my place. We'll order a pizza," Josh said, dialing his car phone as he drove around the block to P Street and pulled into a parking space.

He carried the dog up the stairs to the front door of his place, an elegant old Victorian mansion broken into three apartments, and she followed. She remembered admiring the huge magnolia tree in the yard and also the green door, with its shining brass handle shaped like a bald eagle. Surprising, she thought now, that she hadn't run into Josh once in the past two years.

Unlocking the front door and another one down the hall, he led her up two flights of stairs to his own apartment and switched on the lights.

The small entryway was lit by a two-tiered chandelier. The living room opened to the left, where two big couches stood on either side of a massive fireplace. A beautiful seascape hung above the marble mantelpiece. An oriental screen dominated one wall. "Very tasteful," she said.

"I'm renting it furnished," he replied. "And I'm not crazy about that oriental screen. Those storks don't look real. Their necks are too short. Let's go in the kitchen and find him something to eat. He looks starved."

The dog raised grateful eyes as though he understood help and food were at hand. Darcy glanced back at the storks. They looked right to her, and Josh's strong opinion reminded her that working with him wasn't going to be easy.

The kitchen was long and narrow with a black-and-white tiled floor. Carefully setting the dog down, Josh called his sister about the new plan, then began rummaging through his freezer. Darcy sat at the round oak kitchen table, checked the phone book and dialed the Humane Society.

No luck. It seemed the shelter was closed for the weekend. "Try the Georgetown Vets," Josh suggested, rolling up his shirtsleeves.

Strong hard forearms. She turned away and dialed the number. "They won't be open till eleven tomorrow," she reported a moment later, then hearing the beep, left a message: "We have a lost dog. A small mongrel, black, with one front white paw. If you know the owners, please call this number," and she read the number off Josh's phone.

He'd found a small package of hamburger and set it to defrost in the microwave. "Want a beer?" he asked over the electronic buzz. Before she could respond, he handed her a bottle, set his own on the table and bent down to pet the dog.

She watched him curiously. He'd thought nothing about diving under his Jeep to grab the dog, yet he hadn't plunged himself into finding a wife, a woman he could love. And remembering his strange comment about pack rats who discard those dearest to them, she wondered if there was some woman from his past he regretted not marrying. A lost love he pined for.

Josh checked the hamburger package. "Needs another couple of minutes," he said, pressing buttons.

His kitchen was immaculate, as was the rest of the apartment, or what she'd seen of it. He had made enough of her messiness to make her case his place. But it wasn't fair to put herself down when he could obviously afford a cleaning woman. And as a bachelor, he probably didn't spend much time in his own apartment. She swallowed. Washington had a high population of women looking to connect with eligible men and ready to extend invitations. Capitol Hill teemed with good-looking rich smart women who hit the bars at night, hunting. It wasn't her style, but she knew that eligible handsome men like Josh were at a premium. So it wouldn't surprise her one bit if he went from woman to woman, dining out at restaurants, going to fancy nightclubs and... *It really is of no interest to me. None at all.*

The dog wolfed the hamburger down, making little yelping noises as if to express his gratitude. Josh pulled out a chair and sat down next to Darcy.

"He's cute, isn't he?"

"Yes." Darcy grinned. "He'd be cuter if he had a bath."

"We'll let him settle in first. It's been one hell of a night already," Josh said, sprawling in his chair. He swung his gaze to her. "That's a pretty dress you're wearing. I hope it's not ruined. Let's see if we can't dust you off."

Quick as a wink he rose, said, "Excuse me," and flicked his hand across her chest in a rough flurry, raising hot thoughts. *Not so fast. Press down your fingers.*

She reached up and grabbed his hand before she melted. His head bent so close she could smell his aftershave, recognizing it from the interior of the Jeep. As he straightened up, she saw a slow flush cross his face.

"Maybe I should go home and change," she mumbled, dropping his hand and rising from her chair. Her palm burned from his thumb, and she silently cursed her hormones. He stood within touching distance, and the space between them crackled with tension.

She was breathing audibly but couldn't seem to control herself. He looked at his hand, glanced at her chest and pursed his lips slowly, and the idea that he wanted to kiss her breasts whizzed madly through her head. An even crazier notion made her want to push forward and lead his mouth where it wished to go.

Aghast at the direction of her thoughts, she stepped away abruptly and gripped the back of the nearest chair. He grabbed her hand, which was instantly moist.

"Wait," he said. "I was only trying to brush the mud off. In fact, here, come with me." His thumb pressed into her palm as he led her down the hall toward his bedroom.

Oh, she'd been so transparent he must know she wanted him! He pulled her into his bedroom.

She gasped. "This is ridiculous, Josh," she protested. "What are you doing?"

Her voice sounded fine—firm and normal—masking the emotion behind her words. It seemed far from ridiculous for them to be together in his bedroom. A romantic step toward a strongly emotional man-woman thing.

"Wait till you see this," he said, turning her gently toward the mirror above his chest of drawers.

Two muddy handprints decorated her chest. Her hand flew up to brush herself. "Oh, no," she groaned. "This looks as though . . ."

"It does, doesn't it?" he said, and laughed.

"It's not funny," she complained, embarrassed that he had evoked such strong sexual feelings. Her body wanted more, while logic dictated that she stop while she was still in charge of her actions.

"You shouldn't be pawing women you don't even know," she scolded, thinking how good they looked together in the mirror. The strong planes of his face looked more handsome than ever, and his brown eyes twinkled mischievously. "Why are you . . ."

His laughter died. He ran his fingers through his hair. "Oh, come on, Darcy, it's not as though I don't know you, and it isn't as though I tossed you in the shower and soaped you. So why not just relax? I'll get your dress cleaned."

"No thanks. It's cotton and washable. I'll take a cab and go home and wash it." She would clutch the purse to her chest in the cab so the driver wouldn't notice.

"We could wash it here before Billy and Ginger arrive," he said. "I've been stressing the importance of follow-through with my future brother-in-law. Not finding you keeping your appointment will make him even more laid-back than he is."

"Then I'll just borrow one of your shirts and wear it on top of my dress," she said. He didn't think she was going to stand around in her underwear, did he?

But the thought excited her, and her heart beat faster. She imagined the two of them standing naked together....

He was going to touch her, wasn't he? He patted her on the back. Just an offhand gesture, but his face grew immediately intense.

"Let's take another look at the damage," he said, turning her around, making her fully aware of his big brown eyes approving, roaming, appraising.

X-ray eyes. They seemed to penetrate the cotton, and she saw his mouth purse again. She raised her hands, intending to pull his mouth to hers....

Suddenly the dog barked from the kitchen, snapping her back to reality. She stepped back. "So, can I borrow a shirt?"

He was speechless for a minute, then said, "Sure, sure." He flung open his closet door. "Help yourself." With that, he headed for the door. "I'll order a pizza. Anchovies or no anchovies?" he asked as he left the bedroom.

"No anchovies," she called out, staring at the long row of shirts hanging in dry-cleaner plastic. She selected a pale blue one, crinkled it off the hanger and slipped it on. As she buttoned it, she casually took in her surroundings. Her gaze was drawn to the king-size bed with its navy blue comforter.

She wondered if he slept nude or if a Cartwright wore silk pajamas. Without probing into his drawers, she wouldn't know, so she returned to her original idea. He did sleep nude, and that was how she wanted to think of him. Before she closed the closet door, she saw his expensive suits and blazers with crests on the pockets and reminded herself that one of his suits alone probably cost more than her entire wardrobe. They were definitely wrong for each other. And yet everything in his room beckoned. Plain. Masculine. Sexy.

She cast one last look around the room, filing away every detail. He somehow found time to read, judging by the pile of paperbacks on his nightstand. Dick Francis books, most of which she, too, had enjoyed. She went back out into the kitchen. The dog was sleeping, curled up on a large tan pillow, looking as though he hadn't a care in the world. She smiled.

"Nice outfit," Josh said, sitting at the kitchen table. She shrugged.

The doorbell chimed and Josh ran and flung the door open. "Come in, pizza's on the way. I asked for every kind of topping, some on the side, so everyone should be pleased."

Billy was a rugged good-looking man with a cultivated polished manner—he fit in nicely with the Cartwrights. He shook hands affably with Josh and sent a big smile in her direction. "I've heard a lot about you from Ginger, Darcy. We're really excited about your planning our wedding. That picture of you in *Bridal Ideas* magazine didn't do you justice." He was about thirty, Darcy guessed. He moved energetically, but his eyes shifted far too much, too fast.

"What a charming guy," Darcy told Ginger.

"He's my Prince Charming. So cool. Handsome, too. You can see why I love him." Ginger sighed. "And hey, Darcy, that's a stylish outfit." Ginger laughed. "Is that what they're showing in *Vogue* now? The latest Parisian import?"

When Darcy explained how the dress got muddied, Ginger said, "Look, let me wash it. It'll be all done by the time the pizza gets here and we're ready to leave."

Darcy went into the bathroom, took off the dress and put the shirt back on. Ginger, waiting in the hallway, promptly took away the dress to the small laundry room behind the kitchen. Soon Darcy could hear the machine filling and spinning with a *whoosh whoosh* sound.

Josh gave Darcy an approving glance when she came back into the room. "You look great in that shirt," he said.

An intensely deep sexy message in his eyes hooked her, and she allowed her own eyes to caress him briefly before she deliberately glanced away. The man occupying her so fancifully was Josh Cartwright, a man practiced in sending the right signals to get his way. Admiring him for his compassion for the dog did not erase her other suspicions, she reminded herself. He lacked values. Hadn't he warned George that women from her side of the track deserved to be seduced and left high and dry?

That side of him was coming out in the way he addressed Billy. He didn't laugh and joke with him, didn't even converse normally. The little he said, such as "So how's business?" sounded stilted and condescending, and made Billy squirm.

The pizza-delivery man knocked on the door, and Josh ran out, grabbing his wallet. Ginger had set the dining table with fine gold-rimmed china and crystal goblets, placed white linen napkins alongside the plates and lit the candles in the ornate candelabra. It had never occurred to Darcy that anybody ate pizza other than at the kitchen table with stacks of paper napkins and everyday plates.

"So, Billy, are you getting ready to ride a camel to claim your bride?" Darcy asked when they'd sat down to eat.

"I'd ride the biggest ocean wave or the wildest camel to marry Ginger," he said, making his fiancée glow.

Ginger sighed. "Isn't he romantic?"

Josh rolled his eyes. "Reminds me, Billy and I have to finish our talk sometime soon." He placed a couple of anchovies on his pizza slice. Then he removed the onions, one by one, and set them on the edge of the plate. "Billy, I'd like to talk to you in the living room after we finish eating."

"Sure." Billy smiled. "What do you have in mind?"

"Oh, we can start off with the guest list," Josh said affably enough, but with an edge Darcy didn't miss.

"Let's invite the relatives in Australia," Billy said enthusiastically. "I'd like to meet them. Maybe they'll give us a kangaroo for a wedding gift. Wouldn't that be fun?"

Ginger roared with laughter, but Darcy caught Josh's expression. It said, *Aha, Billy's always looking for a handout, a gift.* It just went to show how worried Josh was about people's motives. To lighten his mood, Darcy added, "Well, at least a kangaroo won't need a suitcase."

Billy and Ginger jumped in with their own spin-offs on a kangaroo's built-in luggage. Nothing really funny, just a way of passing the time pleasantly, but Josh didn't join in. And he hardly ate, either.

"Got to go," Billy said, rising. "I promised my daughter I'd help her with her Girl Scout project."

Josh's shoulders stiffened and his jaw tightened. He set his half-eaten pizza slice down and wiped his fingers savagely on his napkin.

"But that's not due till next week," Ginger protested—till she caught the flirtatious secret look her fiancé cast her. Billy grabbed her purse and tossed it to her. Ginger caught it with a giggle and rose quickly.

"Darcy, I'll call you about the carpets and tents and all that. Hope you get to keep the dog. And Josh, thanks for the pizza." She moved like a hurricane, scraping their plates off as though they were cheap plastic and stashing them in the dishwasher.

Josh slowly stood up, anger whitening his face. "Well, when are we going to talk, Billy? You're always booked up, and I'm telling you, we need to have our conversation."

"We will, we will," Billy replied, edging away. "Thanks for the pizza." He turned to Darcy. "It's going to be a pleasure working with you. Hope to see you soon."

After the couple left, Josh swore under his breath, opened the front door as if to run after them, but at last slammed it shut.

"Now you've met him," he said, sinking back into his chair, face tense.

Darcy's heart contracted. Josh worried like a child, eyebrows lowered, shoulders slumped, mouth in a pout. She wanted to reach out and comfort him, run her finger across his mouth, tell him his sister was a grown-up and he had to let go. He couldn't be responsible for her forever. But he seemed so unreachable.

Josh sat silently, frowning, eating his pizza, carefully arranging the anchovies on his second slice, sprinkling oregano in swirls. Darcy ate silently, watching the dog and feeling Josh's tension and wishing she had answers that would chase his worries away.

Finally he spoke. "Billy is ten years older than Ginger. He's got an ex-wife and two kids."

"Sounds like a lot of people I know," Darcy said.

"Child-support payments," Josh said with contempt. "He's a man who definitely needs money. Lots of it."

Darcy knew then that her assumption was correct. Josh saw Billy Melrose as a gold digger. But he had put her in that category once and perhaps still did. She didn't see Billy that way. He loved Ginger, regardless of her money but people with money were always suspicious of those without any, especially if they wanted to marry one of their own.

Hearing the washing machine come to a groaning halt, Darcy rose. "Ah, at last it's done. Now I can toss it in your dryer," she said, walking through the kitchen into the closet-sized laundry room.

"Let me show you—it's an old dryer," he called out from the dining room and walked behind her into the cramped space standing so close his sleeve brushed hers. "This machine is a real dinosaur. If I planned to stay here forever, I would insist they replace it."

"Here, I'll get my dress out," she said, moving to the washing machine, highly conscious of his masculine presence.

Her moving away barely distanced her from him. She smelled his breath, spiced up with oregano, and felt it graze her shoulders as he leaned over her. Her heart began to pound madly, making her body long to get closer to him; she had the urge to rub her head against his chest.

He leaned closer. Draping an arm around her, he reached into the machine for her dress, and instantly everything beyond his arms receded. She felt him flattened across her back and sighed, unable to will herself to push away his hard body. His head dipping into the crook of her neck touched her skin as softly as a moonlit breeze on a summer night.

"Now, I'll show you how this dryer works. There's a trick to yanking this knob," he said.

An urgent need to nestle into him swept through her. Then he straightened, and emptiness descended on her, making her yearn for the return of his warmth.

"I have to shut the washing-machine door or the stupid dryer won't work," he said.

She obligingly moved out of his way, leaning against the dryer. Leaving the tiny room would have involved rudely pushing past him, abandoning the domestic scene that so tantalized her. He held her wet dress, collected in a big wad, and the sight of it in his hands was so wonderfully intimate her breathing became ragged. She managed to move a few inches away, or maybe she merely shifted from one foot to the other.

He placed the dress in the dryer and slammed the door. She could breathe easier now, end the tension by walking out past him. But instead of moving away and making room, he turned toward her, smiling, his mouth so sexy she wanted to hear him say her name. But his silence carried its own sensual message. He wrapped her up in his gaze and her knees weakened.

Then he spoke. "There's another trick this dryer's known to play. It overcycles, so clothes dry fast, but it can also rip them unless I keep checking."

She only half listened. The words didn't matter. She knew he wanted to kiss her, and a little song hummed a happy tune within her. Her lips moved, softly, to the music.

He leaned over and brushed her lips with his. The kiss was too fleeting, too fast. She wanted him to do it again, but though he breathed harder and his thigh rested on hers, he lifted the lid of the dryer. On some plain of consciousness, she knew he would kiss her again, but that didn't prepare her for his passion when he finally did. A textural symphony that made her cling to him, playing to the music, returning his kiss, exploring his offered mouth.

She could feel his heart beat against hers as he fit his thigh more closely to her. His bulging desire pressed into her, telling her what she already knew: he wanted her badly and wanted her now. He leaned over her again and lifted the lid. This time, he grazed her breast and she arched her back, hoping to get a hold of herself so she could say something cool like "Excuse me." But the words had disappeared into the cotton-candy fluff that swirled around her brain.

He closed his eyes and held her to him, leaning her back against the dryer, which started up with a lusty groan. She felt the machine heave as he kissed her cheek, and its vibrations swiveled her hips so he was rocking on her, with her, in a sexy tempo. He pressed her farther back, against the heat, the throbbing, the intimacy that increased her erotic sensations to form demanding words—*Love me, show me*. She trembled and he clutched her tighter, his hard body rocking against her thighs. Her breath went ragged and her breasts ached against his chest, tight and ready for more specific immediate attention.

She saw tenderness in his eyes, a need to please and take pleasure without alarming her, and a certain mischievousness concerning their erotic prop.

"Great to see you again, Darcy," he whispered, and his breath swept like the wild wind through her cleavage. "I'm sorry you had to settle for pizza."

She tried to move away, but instead, she managed to heighten the physical contact. Her hand touched his face and she traced his lips. He closed his eyes and kissed her finger. Swaying against the dryer, she felt his arms pulsing as he simply held her. His cheek settled against hers, soft and gentle. Then he kissed her lightly on the cheek, and she could feel his heart beat against her own. About to turn her face and taste his lips, she felt the dryer go still behind her. *This is madness. Utter insanity to like it so much.* And with *him*, of all people. She tried to push him away, but he held her firm, gently placing his cheek next to hers, creating a mix of velvet and silk perfumed with spices.

"Darcy, we're two adults . . ."

She turned her back to him, breaking the embrace. She was panting, embarrassed by how much she'd enjoyed this rocking together on the dryer. He naturally wanted to bring them physical satisfaction by continuing somewhere else, or maybe by running the dryer through another cycle.

He let her move away, though, making room for her, rubbing the back of his hand to his lips.

She walked back into the kitchen and saw the dog sleeping, two front paws stretched forward, black and white, and she sat down to let her throbbing heart settle, trying not to think of how Josh caused her to want him. She stood up once, to go to him, then sank back down again. This madness had to stop.

After a few minutes, when Josh emerged holding her dress, her heart started pounding again.

"Thanks," she said, and rose to take it from him.

"Are you sure?" he asked with so much anticipation in his eyes she turned away and grabbed the dress.

No. Not sure at all.

Silently she went into the washroom and locked the door. If he followed, she knew she would press her thigh against his. Both thighs. As she changed into the dress, still warm from the dryer and smelling of lemon from the freshener, she thought she heard his footsteps approaching down the hall and her heart began pounding, *Yes, yes, yes.*

She held her breath, but he didn't knock on the door. She folded his shirt carefully, sliding her hand across it, running her finger over and under the collar. At last she came out of the washroom, and he followed her silently to the front door.

At the door he gently placed his hand on her shoulder. "We'll have to continue our detective work for the dog tomorrow," he said.

As his eyes moved over her, seeking a totally different type of information, she wanted to race for her car.

4

CONTROLLING HER PHYSICAL urges brought a sense of triumph that was still with her the next day. The fact that she'd enjoyed his sexy closeness bothered her, but she had not allowed him to seduce her. She couldn't let her guard down again. There was work to do.

She called the lawyers in Phoenix only to discover that other buyers had entered the picture, two of them serious.

She hung up with a sinking heart. The hardware store sat on a prime parcel of land and carried a hefty price tag. A nearby hotel had sent the price skyrocketing. When Darcy's father and her aunt June were growing up, the land on which DB Hardware sat connected up to nothing but miles of untamed desert where the cacti ruled and the sun beat down unmercifully.

From what her father and aunt had told her, the store had carried a little bit of everything—the usual hardware items, as well as fabric, grain and horse tack. But the depression wiped everyone out, and her grandfather lost his beloved store to a local tycoon. His dying wish was to buy it back, and his two children promised him they would. Whenever her dad and Aunt June talked about DB Hardware, Darcy pictured days full of simple pleasures, and she, too, yearned to revive them.

Now, much as she hated to give her father the bad news, she called him. He said hello and then wheezed into the phone. He tried to cover it up with a chuckle and ended up coughing uncontrollably.

"Dad, I know how much you spent on me," she said, referring to the big wedding that didn't come off.

"You've already paid that back, Darcy."

"I know. But the price of the land has gone sky-high. We have to take action and we don't have much time left. I just called the lawyer and he told me they have two serious buyers."

Her father groaned. "We know how much our house will get, and even with June's savings, it still doesn't amount to half of what we need. Then we have Uncle Albert to take care of. The nursing home isn't cheap. And we don't know if we can take that hardware store and turn it around to make a profit."

"But I believe you can. Look, Dad, you built up Green's Lumberyard. You know the business. I'll go to the bank today."

"Darcy, don't pressure yourself. I'm talking to two or three interested parties, customers, who might want to invest in it as a business. So that's good news."

She hung up thinking how depressed her father sounded. The prospect of investors didn't lighten his load. At fifty, he needed new business challenges, something he could settle into for the rest of his life. She dialed the bank.

Mr. Waters at the MacArthur Savings and Loan agreed to see her. She quickly typed changes on the financial statement, printed it out and, with a burst of new energy, ran to her car and drove down to the bank, hoping and praying.

Mr. Waters kept a pristine office, except for a collection of small frogs made out of wood and iron and glass.

"I love those frogs. How long have you been collecting them?" she asked.

He ignored her attempt at friendly conversation. "I know how it is to want a loan, Miss Blair. Did you bring the information about, uh, Dreams, Inc., with you?"

Darcy handed over the document, hoping to establish her company's profit margin, which now included the Cartwright account. "We're fortunate. *Bridal Ideas* gave us some great publicity. We're projecting a business increase—"

"The bank evaluates the current bottom line, Miss Blair. Let me take a look at the numbers here."

As he read, typing on his computer, she counted his frogs. Thirty-nine. The green ones were prettier than the black, and the biggest frog reminded her of his owner, the banker, with a broad jaw and eyes that popped. Realizing that was unkind of her, she stared out his window. The magnolia tree tumbled pink flowers, like starbursts, against the blue spring sky. Her father had talked about the grapefruit tree his mother had planted next to the store in Phoenix and how she'd drawn precious water from a tiny stream to keep it going. It never bore fruit, and Darcy thought of how someday, her father would plant another grapefruit tree in his mother's honor in the same spot.

At last the banker looked up. "I'm afraid my position on the loan hasn't changed."

In other words, she couldn't get a loan based on present business. She left his office hating frogs.

Back at her own office, Darcy found a pale Aunt June holding her wrist, a sure sign her carpel tunnel had flared up again. Darcy didn't want to burden her with bad news.

"You look like you're hurting, Aunt June. Why don't you go home and take your medication?"

"I can't. We have the Jamaica bash to cater." Aunt June massaged her neck with one trembling hand. "People are really into the island motif this year."

"I'll take over for you. Don't worry." Darcy ushered the elderly woman out, silencing her protests. "Planning island parties always puts me in a good mood. I think of golden beaches. Squawking parrots. Palm trees dropping coconuts. It sounds so warm and friendly." But if truth be known, little could excite her at the moment.

"Josh Cartwright is on the phone for you," Amy said over the intercom. Darcy's heart fluttered.

"How's the dog?" were her first words.

He laughed. "What a way to greet a guy. I'm fine, thank you. So is the dog. I haven't turned up anything yet. You know, he got in bed with me last night. Curled up. I think he misses you."

An image of Josh, naked in bed, filled her thoughts.

"Are you there?"

"Sorry," she said. "I was trying to think of who else to call. Maybe I'll run an ad in the *Georgetowner*." She clutched at ideas to abate the wild flow of excitement rushing through her.

"Do you want me to do it?"

"Oh, yes."

She felt heat rushing up to her face. She took a deep breath. "No. I can place the ad. I'll do it right now. Bye."

The phone rang again. "It's me again. Are you free tonight?"

"No, Josh. I . . . we're catering a Jamaican party and, in fact, we're busy all week." The excuse had sprung up just in time.

She heard him sigh. "The dog would like to see you."

Darcy laughed. "Tell him woof, woof. That's short for I miss you, too."

"Okay." He chuckled. "I'll do that." There was a long pause before he added, "And have fun at your party."

She hung up the phone thinking that he had actually sounded genuinely disappointed. She smiled and ran her fingers through her hair, daydreaming until the bustle outside her door reminded her she had work to do. Tons of it. And no time to fritter away with a self-centered handsome man who saw her as some sort of challenge. Given his lady-killer image, she was sure he played the numbers. Called woman after woman. Hadn't he flirtatiously tried to catch her eye at every party she'd attended with George? She remembered him actually jumping out of his chair to get her a drink, and she'd felt flattered until George told her what a flirt Josh Cartwright was.

He was the kind of man who didn't much care for anything but the chase. He had to learn to take no for an answer.

THE CITY PLANNER, who wanted the ski-slope wedding had actually called, and Darcy's spirits soared all week. They weren't ready to talk budget just yet, but a prospect was better than none and the call confirmed the woman's genuine interest. Darcy also took comfort in landing two small catering jobs. They didn't pay as much as wedding planning but would take care of the rent for the next month and add to the Dreams, Inc., list of clients.

On this Friday night, after declining dinner with Martin, she'd gone to bed thinking of Josh curled up with the mutt. He had called a couple of times during the week to tell her the dog remained unclaimed. But he picked the worst times to call, and she had been polite but brief.

Saturday morning the phone jangled Darcy rudely out of sleep. It was Josh.

"I bathed him and he looks good. I'm talking about our dog."

Our dog? She plumped the pillows and leaned back. "Really?" she said, rubbing her eyes. "Did you see any injuries?" The bedside clock said it was seven.

"No. He's thin underneath all that unclipped fur. And obviously he's been bathed before, because he didn't seem to mind it. But this morning, he isn't crazy about canned food so I'm going to get a variety of chow."

"I'm glad he's doing well. The ad went in. If you'd like me to, I'll call Georgetown Vets again and any other place I can think of," Darcy said, brimming with energy.

"Great," he said. "After I get the dog food, I'll stop by and pick you up, and you can make the calls from here."

"That's not..." Darcy began, but couldn't finish. She wanted to see the dog. And Josh. There were questions about the wedding. She had nothing else pressing today, and it would be nice to get away from her small apartment. "Okay, I'll be ready in an hour."

When she hung up, she moved to the window. It was a beautiful day. The tulips and hyacinths had burst forth into a spectacular patch of red and blue in the courtyard, and the birds were singing. Glad she hadn't slept the spring morning away, she began getting ready, thinking of Josh's velvet voice, how much he cared for the stray.

In the shower, with the warm water pulsing over her, she felt filled with excitement. She wanted to touch him, hold his hand, tell him she'd be there for him for Ginger's wedding and not to worry so much about Billy.

She emerged from the shower setting firm rules for seeing Josh. Stick to the topic of the dog. Safe. Detached. That was the only way to prevent being hurt, she thought, turning on her hair dryer.

He'd occupied her thoughts so much she had forgotten to check her messages last night when she'd arrived home late and exhausted. The answering machine light blinked red, and setting down her hair dryer, she hit the play button. There was a message from Antonio Constantino, a carpet-store owner and family friend, whom she'd called about renting oriental carpets for Ginger's wedding. Antonio was her dad's buddy and her unofficial godfather.

He said, "You can come on Saturday evening after hours, since I don't want the reputation of renting. I will be honored to show you carpets, Miss Darcy, at seven-thirty."

Darcy was delighted. Antonio Constantino, the best-known carpet dealer in Washington, D.C., was going to break his rules for once. Oriental rugs had fascinated her from the first day she'd gone into Antonio's shop and seen those rich tropical pinks and blues, geometrics and flowers that spoke of faraway places and gardens soaked in the sun. And although Josh had not stipulated renting them, she knew buying them would cost a bundle. And saving money for clients always pleased her, even if they had a limitless budget.

By the time Josh rang her doorbell she was ready, wearing jeans and a red shirt with a blue cotton pull-over draped across her shoulders. He smiled broadly and led her to his Jeep, talking about the dog, while she observed how well his jeans emphasized his long legs and the white shirt set off his rugged face. As he opened the door for her, the excitement in his eyes drew her further into the promise of adventure of the new day.

"In the middle of the night the dog jumped on the bed again." Josh's eyes locked with hers. "I think he missed you," he said, and her heart leapt, even as she cautioned herself that he specialized in pouring on the charm.

Josh lived only about ten minutes by car from her. Going up the steps, Darcy was painfully aware of the contrast between their apartments. His was on the right side of the tracks. The house next door to his had once belonged to Jackie O's stepfather. The house across the street was where the very wealthy senator from North Carolina lived. The area where these stately homes stood was on all the tourist maps; by contrast, her own neighborhood could be called "nowhere land," where nobody important lived.

Now here she was crossing the tracks, going up those steps. Josh took his mail from a locked brass mailbox in the marbled entrance hall. The gleam of polished brass, the sparkle of the chandelier, underscored the fact that his was a fancy address that served as a spider's web for people like her. She must never forget that. And, she told herself, if it wasn't for the dog, she wouldn't be here this minute. Having found the animal together, they shared equal responsibility for it.

As she stepped into his apartment, the dog came bounding up to her with such enthusiasm she delightedly bent down and patted him. "We'll find your owner soon," she said tenderly. "You look handsome all groomed. Nice and shiny."

"If we don't find his owner, would you like to have him?" Josh asked.

The offer took her by surprise. "I'd love to, but they don't allow pets in my building," she said. No sooner were the words out of her mouth than they heard a knocking on the door.

Opening it, Josh said, "Darcy, this is our building super. Anything wrong?" he asked the man.

"I'm looking at a problem." The super, a stocky older fellow, pointed at the barking dog Darcy was holding back. "You know the building rules, Mr. Cartwright."

"But he's not living here. He's just waiting for his owner." Josh went on to explain how they'd found the dog and what efforts they were making to locate his owners.

"He better be out of here today," the super said. "Or we'll have to implement Code Three." Then he turned and left.

Holding the dog in her arms, Darcy asked, "Code Three? Does that mean forced eviction of dog, or dog and owner?"

"It probably means both, plus a sizable bribe," Josh sighed. "It's too early to start calling. Let's have some coffee."

The percolator was bubbling away in the kitchen, spreading a nice warm smell of freshly ground java. Darcy sat down, still holding the dog, who smelled of herbal shampoo. She couldn't remember ever having cuddled a dog; it wasn't so hard, after all.

Josh's kitchen, in broad daylight, showed his personal touch. Piles of red paper plates. Carryout menus tacked on a bulletin board. An old program for the Washington Symphony Orchestra. A tennis racquet. Designer sunglasses. A handful of change. Phone numbers scrawled on a piece of paper.

"I've called Ginger and Billy to come and join us, but he's a slippery one." Josh sighed. "This morning he has to take one of his sons to a baseball game. I thought divorced fathers only saw their kids part of the time, but Billy seems to see them constantly." He frowned as he splashed the coffee in their cups.

"He must like being a father," she said, trying not to think of the dryer in the tiny room next door and how she'd wanted Josh to lean on her forever.

Josh slammed a cupboard door. "Sure does, and Ginger wants to have at least three kids." He rolled his eyes. "'It will be the family I never had,' she keeps saying. She's too young to . . ." He sat down and spooned sugar into his coffee so forcefully the cup wavered dangerously.

"Don't you like kids?" she asked, surprised that a man who showed so much kindness to a stray dog wouldn't understand Billy's need to be with his children.

He looked wistful. He sighed, started to say something, then changed his mind. "Oh, I wouldn't mind a houseful of kids," he said much too casually, leaving her undecided as to whether he was joking. But from what he had said about Ginger a minute ago, she figured he didn't want any children at all.

"I'll call the Humane Society," he said, looking up the number in the phone book.

While he made the call, Darcy jotted down numbers of vets and pet stores. They took turns playing with the dog and calling—with no luck. Each time Josh leaned against the counter, a wish to do some leaning on *him* came into her mind. The man conveyed sex appeal even when he wasn't attempting to flirt. Surely this was one reason George envied Josh. She considered asking Josh about his friendship with George, but then Josh spoke.

"Since this poor mutt must have traveled quite far, let's call the neighboring suburban vets in Virginia and Maryland," Josh suggested, and they began the process again.

Listening to him talk on the phone, Darcy heard real compassion in his tone. "Please ask your colleagues.

Maybe someone's at the desk right now upset about this dog." And it tugged at her heart while raising questions. Why had he rejected himself as father material? Why wasn't he married?

As for her, not ever having children was the only regret she harbored against her vow not to marry. Becoming a surrogate mother had crossed her mind when she saw the topic in the news. But she could never give up a baby.

George loved children and she'd liked his jolly teasing of his sister's kids. She and George had talked about having three, about living in a rambling old house with a fireplace. Anger and hurt swept through her again.

Josh was talking to Ginger on the portable phone now and had wandered off into the living room. She folded the nearest paper napkin slowly into an arrow and let it flutter from her fingers onto the table in front of her. It landed with the point toward her. She snatched it up and crumpled it. Yes, she was to blame for believing George, even if he had made it all sound so totally believable. She'd loved George for his upbeat mischievous ways and should have known he liked to spin stories and dreams. But to the point of taking her to the altar?

Water under the bridge, except this water tumbled huge waves of anguish over her even now. She hadn't drowned, though, and she wouldn't ever take the risk of trusting a charming man again.

One-thirty rolled around, and they still hadn't located any information on the foundling. "I have errands to run," Darcy said. "I'll grab a cab home." Making a mental list of her errands—dry cleaner, grocery store, post office—Darcy remembered Antonio's call.

"The carpet-shop owner offered to open up his shop at seven-thirty this evening to show me a selection of carpets he's willing to rent," she said. "He doesn't do this sort of thing normally, so if Ginger is available, let's do it."

While he called Ginger and left a message on her machine, she flung her purse over her shoulder and stood poised to run out for a cab.

"Wait, I'll drive you," he said. She protested and he insisted. "There's no reason on earth for you to take a cab or walk. In fact, I'll buy you lunch."

"Can't do lunch. I have too many things to do," she said as they walked to his Jeep. The intense search for the dog's owners had put their togetherness on a more impersonal level, and Darcy felt relieved. She had spent too much time last night wondering what it would have been like if she had gone with her feelings and let him make love to her. And that type of dreaming could only lead to heartache.

Stopped at a traffic light, he shot her an intense look. Excitement filled her again. Then he reached for her hand and massaged her cold palm, making it warm and moist. She pulled her hand away and fiddled with her seat belt.

"Thanks for helping with the dog," he said. She sat speechless, overtaken with a need for his kiss. *Am I so lonely?*

As they got to her street, his car phone rang and she noticed how his breezy greeting changed to a brisk discussion about a legal case. "I'll try to answer your questions," he said, voice and manner on guard.

Josh's expression as he listened on the phone, the square set to his shoulders, the firm way his lips were clamped together, suddenly reminded her of the way he'd acted when, dressed in her wedding gown, she'd tried to find out the whereabouts of George.

She wondered why he hadn't made any reference to what had happened to George. What had made the man she loved turn away from her? Josh and George were still friends, weren't they? And what on earth was she doing worrying about a stray dog and riding around with a man connected to George? And feeling horny?

"You feeling okay?"

She hadn't realized Josh was off the phone. She did know that he had pulled up alongside her car but as she reached for the door handle, he pulled her hand away toward him.

"What put you in such a bad mood? What's going on?"

"Well . . ." she began uncertainly. "It is odd that we haven't talked about . . ."

"George." He sighed. "It's been on my mind."

"Oh?"

"I'm really sorry about what happened. I did try to call you several times."

"Why didn't you tell me George wasn't going to show up?"

He looked uneasy. His face turned red. "I . . . uh, didn't know for sure."

"You had your suspicions, though."

He started to speak, changed his mind, glanced at her, then away. He cleared his throat. "Look. That's all in the past. It has nothing to do with today and us."

So that's all he's going to say, she thought, judging by his silence over five long infernal minutes. *Damn him.* She flung the door open and climbed out of the Jeep.

"Wait, Darcy."

She stopped, grasping at her professional side. Finally she said, "I'll see you and Ginger at the carpet shop."

5

JOSH DROVE to his office on Pennsylvania Avenue, disturbed that Darcy would still be so deeply interested in George. Didn't she understand that she'd been lucky?

He got on the elevator to go up to his office but continued to travel back in time. At that joyless reception, following the wedding that never took place, Josh remembered standing at the bar, wishing he could find some way of comforting her, erasing the pain from her lovely face. He remembered that powerful urge to marry her himself, and now he was glad he hadn't made a fool of himself. He remembered trying to think of just the right words to ease her heartbreak without totally sacrificing his loyalty to George. But his brain had turned as soggy as the stuffed mushroom he had returned to the gilt-edged plate.

As best man, he felt responsible for Darcy's pain. He should have told her that, when he drove George home after the rowdy drunken bachelor's party the night before the wedding, a redhead was waiting outside his apartment door. She'd sprung forward at seeing George, crying, "He's agreed to a divorce. I'm free to marry you!"

"One of her jokes." George had winked at him, but then clasped her like a drowning man. "Let's go inside and I'll propose properly," he'd said to her, so absorbed in her embrace that he forgot Josh standing there.

The memory of that episode aggravated the nerve in his jaw. He'd always known George as a man of strong appetites when it came to eating, drinking, gambling and women. But, having done a little of that himself, he had chalked it all up to an urge to sow wild oats. He should have taken charge and slapped some sense into George, followed through to get George to admit his intentions before beautiful innocent Darcy even got herself dressed for the wedding.

Josh sighed and frowned. He remembered his anger with George and with himself. He remembered squeezing the stem off his wineglass. He remembered how the glass had shattered with a little *ping* and how the waiter had run up with a wad of napkins. Absent-mindedly Josh sucked his right index finger, just as he'd done then.

His in basket was overflowing. Sitting at his desk, he speed-read, signed a few memos his secretary had typed up, read through a report and checked his e-mail.

After collecting the files his associates had left him on an ongoing case, he went home, thinking what a lonely place home could be. The thought that at least he was going to see Darcy at the carpet shop brightened his mood.

The noise of traffic and airplanes hit him as he emerged from the office building, and he squinted into the bright light. As he turned to walk to his office down the block, he heard a loud hello, swung around and saw a brunette waving frantically. He recognized Amanda Loch, Ginger's best friend, crossing the parking lot, dressed in a red jumpsuit. He grinned and kissed her on the cheek.

"How're you holding up planning Ginger's wedding?" she asked. "She told me how supportive you are."

He grinned again, pleased that Ginger didn't consider his heavy involvement as meddling. He had worried about Ginger turning away from him and his suspicions of Billy. And some days, he did wonder if he wasn't way off the mark. Still, as his sister's only relative, he had to check her future husband out.

He'd thought he knew Ginger well until this past year when she suddenly seemed so grown-up. She had developed a mysterious womanly quality he didn't understand, and it all had to do with her selection of the love of her life.

But there were some things about Darcy he didn't understand, either. Her taste in men. Why had she agreed to marry a man like George? She hadn't said one negative thing about Billy, either. And if she couldn't see Billy's faults, how could she see his own attributes? He had so much to give her. But she was still hung up on George, and until she resolved that, he wasn't going to get anywhere with her.

He wanted to wrap himself around Darcy and make such mad passionate love to her she would never look at another man again. He needed to undress her slowly. He needed to . . . He took his hurting body to his apartment, glad nobody was around.

Once inside he hurried to the kitchen, where he had left the dog. "Hello pooch," He patted the happy animal, opened a can of dog food and set down a heaping bowl. Then he turned to his answering machine.

No messages awaited him regarding the stray at his apartment. Josh sat at the kitchen table, sorting and tossing his mail, listening to the dog making greedy little noises as he ate. He was probably feeding him too much, but the poor thing seemed positively starved.

His own stomach growled and he wished there were leftovers from a home-cooked meal. But his cooking didn't go beyond defrosting frozen foods. He popped a slice of bread into the toaster and waited. And waited. Finally he realized the element wasn't on although the toaster was plugged in. Rattling the toaster around didn't get any action. He swore out loud. He had no idea how to fix it. And that frustrated him no end. He ate the untoasted bread with butter on it, hating that he hadn't inherited the mechanical skills of his father, who supposedly could fix everything from television sets to cars. If he couldn't fix things, how could he hope to fix his love life? How could he make Darcy understand how much he wanted her?

Damn, he'd almost forgotten the tennis game with his law partner, Ted Dawson. Josh changed into his tennis whites, grabbed his racquet and raced away. Dawson and his wife had also invited him to a party tonight to meet a woman engineer they'd raved about. He would have to find a polite way to get out of that. The status of eligible bachelor had its downside, and he'd been stuck going downhill for far too long.

What he wanted to do tonight was look at the carpets, then talk Darcy into dinner. He wasn't going to take no for an answer. He'd seen her thawing out over the dryer. Remembering her vibrating body against his, he sighed. He should have lifted her bodily and set her on the dryer, then kissed and caressed her and fulfilled their desires. Just the thought of what could have been was making him so hot he almost drove right by the tennis courts.

BY THE TIME she'd run her errands, grabbed a salad and changed into a marigold-print summer dress, Darcy was running a little late. And hating the thought of seeing Josh Cartwright, she arrived flustered at Constantino's shop.

"Miss Darcy, it's a pleasure to see you again. Come in and sit down," the old bearded man said. "Mr. Cartwright has been rather worried about you."

Josh was standing to her left. Startled, Darcy said, "Oh, hi. I'm sorry I was delayed. Who would have thought buying stamps would take twenty minutes? Where's Ginger? And how's the dog?"

"Dog misses you. Ginger couldn't make it. Something to do with getting Billy's car fixed while he's working," Josh replied with a weary shrug and a displeased shake of his head.

"If you like, I can show you the carpets next Sunday." Antonio's offer was made with such hesitation it was clear he considered that an imposition. "Only for Miss Darcy. I have had the good fortune of knowing her parents for a long time." He smiled. "You were a pretty little girl and you sang like a bird."

Darcy felt herself turn red. That singing phase of hers, where she dreamed of being a star, had been so ridiculous.

"You want to see the carpets on Sunday?" Antonio asked.

"Yes, we can come back then," Darcy agreed quickly. "We're very appreciative of your offer."

"Wait. We can't do it next Sunday. I might be out of town. Or Ginger might have something come up," Josh said urgently. "Why don't we look through and settle the whole carpet issue now?"

"Very well then. This way please." Antonio led them into a large hall with rolls and rolls of carpets as thick as pillars leaning against the walls. He waved a solicitous hand toward two sofas arranged at one end.

Darcy and Josh sat together on a sofa. Antonio excused himself, saying, "I will return."

"You look great," Josh said, casting a sweeping look at her colorful dress.

She smiled, trying not to stare at the dark hair peeping out through the open collar of the white shirt he wore with his khaki slacks. "It's cold in here," she said.

Josh slid his arm off the back of the sofa and she moved away quickly.

Antonio returned carrying a loaded silver tray, set it on the coffee table and explained, "We have to run the air-conditioning higher than normal to keep the carpets from developing a musty mildew odor from the humidity. But I can offer you a shawl."

"Oh, no, it's not that cold," Darcy said. "And the mint tea will warm me up in a hurry. It smells wonderful."

The old man nodded. He poured two cups of the steaming hot liquid. "We will begin now," he said. "What colors would you like to see?"

Josh turned to Darcy. "Go ahead. What would you like?"

She blushed and was angry with herself for doing so. Assuming her most businesslike tone, she said, "Since Ginger's not here, why don't you tell us what *you* like?"

"This color," Josh said, reaching over and touching Darcy's dress, tracing a marigold with his finger. "Do you have any carpets in this color?"

Darcy outwardly ignored the fact that his tracings were causing her to have naughty thoughts.

Antonio said, "Yes, sir. Although you will find yellow is not a predominant color. Nothing here is solid. The patterns are varieties of Persian gardens or geometrics of ancient tiles. So this beautiful color will be combined with others in harmony. And I have a most beautiful collection."

"What do you think?" Josh asked Darcy.

"I love the color," she said, playfully patting her dress.

Antonio lumbered over to one pile of carpets, then moved to check those rolled up against the wall. Then he lifted one over his shoulder and plopped it on the floor. Unrolling it, he said, "Now this carpet has the finest silk. Handmade. But I can only offer it for sale and not for lease."

Winking at Josh, Darcy helped herself to a diamond-shaped candy. It practically melted in her mouth. Buttery with a delicious nutty flavor. Seeing Josh reach for a candy pleased her. His willingness to try different foods spoke of him as an adventurous eater. Like the man pictured sucking on an olive in that erotic book, Josh devoted his full attention to the candy. His mouth curved in that incredibly sexy way. He might as well have said her name aloud, called her from a mountaintop. She was ready to run and climb him.

Antonio was talking, saying something about the movie that was going to be filmed on the C&O Canal where Key Bridge crossed it and the Potomac. She tried to pay attention, find out the name of the movie she hadn't heard about, but only one thought engrossed her. *How adventurous is he in his lovemaking?*

Wild hot images of Josh caressing her bare skin against the carpet spread an incredible longing through her. A picture of him pressing himself on her until the silky pattern transferred itself to her back was making her breathe hard. Sexy tattooing. If she could have her way, lovemaking carpets would become a big hit. People could put them on their beds, on the floor or on the grass. Anywhere and everywhere. These special carpets would have the best texture, inviting yet firm enough to transfer the pattern to skin. Temporary love tattoos. Instant pleasure. Permanent memories. But first she would have to test them out, wouldn't she? Josh could help her find the right texture, the best pattern she could press on his back, herself on top, exploring that mouth and other things. The fact she was indulging in such thoughts increased her agitation.

"I hope the dust in the shop is not affecting you, Miss Darcy," Antonio said. Embarrassed, she shook her head. The carpet dealer proceeded to unroll more carpets, each more exquisite than the last. Darcy could smell the mint from the tea and Josh's musky aftershave, even though they weren't sitting that close. As she reached for another candy, Josh got up, crossed to a carpet and bent down to touch it, then deliberately sat back down closer to her. The brush of his knee made her heart miss a beat, and she hurriedly moved her knee away.

As Antonio launched into another sales pitch, the phone rang. Antonio picked it up, listened and burst into a babble of Greek. Josh and Darcy didn't know exactly what he was saying, but his manner expressed trouble.

"An emergency." Antonio's voice trembled. "I must go home. But please—" his eyes darted wildly "—stay and proceed. Look and select. Mark carpet numbers down." He pointed to a notepad on the table.

"Wait," Josh said. "We can do this another time. Can we help you with your emergency?"

"No. Only God can help. My daughter is in labor. It's too soon. But I must go. The doors will lock automatically behind you."

Before the two of them could react, Antonio was gone. They heard a door slam.

"We should follow him. Surely there's something we can do to help," Josh said, rushing toward the door.

Darcy grabbed her purse and ran, filled with trepidation. Antonio's only daughter's long-awaited pregnancy had brought so much joy and pride to the family. "Dear God, don't let anything happen to her or the baby," Darcy prayed as she caught up with Josh running through the outer showroom toward the front door. "The whole family's been waiting for this day, but the doctors warned them there might be complications," she said.

"I hope everything goes well. I'm sure it will and the baby will arrive in a good family situation. That's so important," Josh tugged at the door handle. He pulled, pushed, twisted it this way and that.

"Normally these doors can be opened from the inside," he said. "There must be a trick to it." Running his hand up the sides of the door, he suddenly paused and backed away, pointing to a battery of blinking red lights way up high above the door. "Quite a sophisticated security system," he said. "This definitely beats the one in our office, and that one's complex enough."

"There should be a phone number somewhere. Maybe there's one in that office," Darcy said, running to a glass cubicle. The door was locked. Then she saw some numbers way up by the blinking lights. "I'll go find a ladder. There should be one around here somewhere."

"Wait, I have a better idea. There's no point in poking around and setting off false alarms when we don't need to."

"What idea?" The question on her lips blew away as Josh scooped her up in his arms. Shocked, she couldn't speak. Snug and warm against him, feeling his warm breath in her hair and his hand on her bottom, she trembled with excitement. He could carry her to his cave or to his carpet. She wanted to ruffle his hair and embrace him, settle deep into the masculine fit she knew would bring her satisfaction. But would it? Wanting and needing could also bring pain. She sighed.

"What're you doing, Josh?" she groaned. "Please set me down." *Set me down before I wrap myself around you.*

He carried her back to the door. "I'm going to hold you up, so you can read the phone number," he said. Then he easily hoisted her up, strong hands gripping her legs.

He made her feel light, feminine, athletic. She had never been able to be hoisted around in gym class, but those exercises lacked the sexual tension that gripped her now. As she clutched his shoulder and straightened, she could feel him breathing hard against the space between her thighs. And her body responded instantly with warm pleasure.

Trying to ignore the steamy sexuality of their positions, she managed to read the numbers aloud. "Six, Four..." Her voice shook unbearably.

He repeated the numbers in a ragged voice, muffled against her dress, stirring deep through the fabric, till she felt his words echo inside her. As his lips moved against her thigh, she wiggled and a low moan escaped her. Holding on to his shoulders, she slid downward, and her breasts crushed first against his face, making her heart almost stop. Then, as his arms enveloped her and her feet hit the floor, she breathed harder against the feel of his desire pushing on her through all the fabric. He had lowered his head to her shoulder and was holding her tight, his hand trembling on her back. His thick hair grazed her face. *This is too deliciously close, too intimate, too scary.*

Darcy stumbled out of his embrace. She recited the phone number. "Let's call before we forget." She mentally clutched at the number. Reality.

"Are you sure it's six, four, two? Wasn't the prefix six, two, four?" he asked, reaching for her hand. "I'd better lift you up again."

"I'm positive," she said, moving out of his reach and crossing to a nearby wall phone.

"Wait," he said in a thick voice. "Do we want to add to Antonio's troubles? Shouldn't we let the poor guy at least get to the hospital before we have the security people paging him, as you know they will? That's the protocol, you know. They're not going to let us out unless they know we were in here at Antonio's invitation."

"For heaven's sake," Darcy muttered, "they won't have to call Antonio. The security people will just let us out." There was some truth to what he was saying, but she could hardly trust herself to be locked up with Josh. She wanted to touch him in the worst possible way in the most private places.

"Think about it. That's not how it works," Josh said.

Darcy grabbed her purse, pulled out the small notebook and pen she always carried with her and jotted down the phone number. "This way, we won't forget," she said, suddenly unsure her memory would hold up.

Josh looked a little wild-eyed. "Okay, then you agree to give Antonio time to check on his daughter?" His hair was rumpled, with the little dark waves cascading every which way. His shirt was pulled down over the shoulder she'd grasped.

"I guess we should look through the carpets and select the ones you want to lease. That'll take a few minutes. Then I'll call his house and see what's up."

"Good idea," Josh said, ambling back to the inner showroom. "He might even remember he locked us in and come back," he added, as though he hoped that wouldn't happen. "You know, I used to dream about getting locked up in a department store with a beautiful woman. Did you ever fantasize about something like that?"

His eyes touched hers briefly, tantalizing her. *Yes. I dreamed your dream, locked up with a handsome man.* "As a child," she said, desperately trying to slow her pulse, "I thought about getting locked up in a candy store."

"Same idea," he said, looking deep into her eyes. "It's exciting. If Antonio were here, he'd call it kismet. Fate has us locked up. If this was a candy store, we would be tasting . . . wonderful tastes."

He reached for her hand and held it to his lips, swirling the softest kiss across her nails. He turned her hand over and kissed her palm in the center, as though reaching for the very center of her being. She quivered and removed her hand from his, feeling a sudden cold loss. Heart beating wildly, she forced herself to speak. "Electronic glitch, not fate," she said.

It surprised her that he didn't gather her in his arms and kiss her. It excited her that he might just do that at any minute. And it did cross her mind that he wanted her to take the lead, and her body supported that idea, telling her to jump him, caress him till he cried out. But she'd never done such a thing in her life. And why would Josh Cartwright, the ladies' man, be holding back from pressing her against the wall and making wild passionate love to her?

She clutched at the thick rough side of a huge roll of carpet propped up against the wall. Anxious to get back to the purpose of their visit and squelch the clamoring from the hungry depths of her soul, she pushed at its thick woolly mass. It was like pushing a mule.

"Here, let me," Josh said, picking up the massive roll as though it were a duffel bag and tossing it on the floor. "I'll play Antonio. If you'll just sit down and have some more tea, Miss Darcy, I will be honored." He grinned and bowed.

Sinking onto the couch, Darcy laughed. Josh had Antonio's bow down pat. She chuckled. "Does this mean you're going to continue trying to sell me these carpets?"

"Absolutely." Josh laughed. Unrolling the carpet, he said, "This pattern, madam, is called the Garden of Eden. As you see, the flowers here are the kind that only grew in the Garden of Eden. That's when the soil and the air were pure. Our best artisans in Mesopotamia wove this in the best tradition of their ancestors. It's the finest wool that Mesopotamian lambs could provide for creating this unforgettable memory."

Darcy couldn't stop laughing. "But it isn't wool," she said, leaning down and touching its nubby surface. "It's papyrus."

Josh blanched for a second, then realizing she was joking, he grinned. "Impossible," he said. "Papyrus is fuzz-free, perpetually washed in the sacred Nile. This is wool."

"It's a gorgeous pattern. Intricate. Geometric. But the rug is too blue," she said, thinking how imaginative he was, how entertaining, how funny. And his tall strong body exuded sexuality, making her heart respond with little tremors.

"Scratch this one," he said, putting it aside and reaching for the next roll. He unfurled it on top of the other one. "Is there any more of that tea left?"

"It's a little cold now but still tasty. Nice way to wash down these candies. I swear I've already put on five pounds stuffing my face like this." Darcy filled Josh's cup.

He sipped at his tea, fitting his lips sensuously around the rim of the glass. Then he said, "Tastes like I'm sucking on a mint leaf." Setting the cup back on the table, he added, "As for gaining weight, you don't have to worry. You're light as air."

She turned red, remembering her breasts against his face and the warmth of his breath between her thighs. And she wished he would hold her again. *Foolish idea.* It wasn't ever going to happen because she wouldn't allow it, even though the press of his desire was fresh in her mind. A small distinct voice—her own—tugged at her business sense to anchor her safely away from such utter madness as to want him for pure sexual pleasure. That only worked in fantasy.

"Ginger should like this one." Darcy spoke desperately, trying to shake off that strong message in his eyes that told her he wanted her and wanted her now. In a tight little voice she went on, "You know, now that you've been here, you can bring Ginger and confirm any selections you make today."

"Ginger?" he asked so absentmindedly that Darcy shot him a surprised look.

Slowly he turned. "Yes. Good idea," he said, voice as thick as molasses. "And since Ginger will have her say, uh, later, why don't you select what you like now?"

Darcy, notebook in hand, walked around the red carpet, flipping up corners, searching for the little white tag with numbers on it.

"This one is quite beautiful. The pattern isn't as busy as most of them. You can see the individual flowers on it. What do you think, Josh?"

"If you like it, I love it," he said.

Startled by the intensity of his voice, she lowered her head and jotted down the number. He fell silent and she wondered if he was tired. Most men didn't have this much patience when it came to shopping.

"Well, Antonio, you're awfully quiet," she teased.

"I'm having second thoughts about the seating. The guests are going to sit on pillows on these rugs? Is that the general plan? We should really check these out for comfort."

"Yes. You have a point, Josh. I suppose most of the guests are not used to sitting on the floor unless they're doing yoga." No one as yet had suggested a yoga wedding, but she smiled at the vision of a hundred guests in the lotus position.

Wishing he would quit looking at her in that sexy way, Darcy picked up two small green silk pillows from the couch and dropped them onto the carpet. She slipped out of her shoes and sat tentatively on a pillow, arranging her skirt modestly around her ankles. As she settled in, the pillow was so soft it waffled down and Darcy laughed nervously as she rolled backward.

Josh knelt with his upper body leaning over her, braced by his hands on either side of her. "Here, let me help you," he said, gazing into her eyes.

Mesmerized, she gazed back, unable to protest. His eyes were tapping into her soul. His presence was sending such deep sexual messages she wanted to pull him down and hold him, feel her breasts crushed against his face as they had been before. But that would be madness, a surefire way to get herself dumped. *Dangerous wishes.*

"I'm okay, I can get up," she said, voice shaky, knees drawn up, as she struggled to rise.

He said nothing and looked away. Heart beating rapidly, she realized he was going to move away and end her torture. She righted herself only to find he didn't intend to move.

She had folded herself into his arms. And he held her gently as though she was the most fragile of possessions. Her breath came in big spurts. Her eyes closed. Her mind filled with the smell of mint mingled with his after-shave and him. She waited for him to touch her, kiss her, press her down on the carpet.

He gently smoothed back her hair. Then, caressing her cheek with his fingers, he sighed, prolonging her torture. She opened her eyes, lowering her head for a closer caress. There was no reason to deny this.

His lips on hers, soft and warm, he cradled her more comfortably in his arms and kissed her again, erasing the world in a mix of masculine textures all around her. She pressed her own textures on his, mingling their passion.

"I've held back too long," he groaned. "I wanted you to be sure you want me."

He slipped his hand across her chest, kissing her neck, tossing a thigh intimately over hers. She kissed his cheek, pressing him to her. He pulled her over, closer to his hard body.

As the geometrics of the carpet came into view, sanity returned. A moment's satisfaction would be sweet, very sweet, but how soon before rejection followed? She had nothing in common with Josh Cartwright, certainly not the ability to roam his upper-class world with ease. She was acting like a teenager, leading him on, wishing for his physical attentions. She pushed him away abruptly and disentangled herself, then stood up.

"I've got to get big pillows. Something with substance so they don't sink so much," she mumbled.

He simply sprawled on the carpet, one arm flung out, hand resting, palm up, inches from her foot. Then he, too, rose and sat down on the couch, brow furled in thought.

"Darcy?" He spoke gruffly. "Why are you leaving me? Come here and let me make love to you."

"It's not right," she sputtered. "I'm not interested in that kind of a relationship."

He started to protest, rising to approach her, but she held up a warning hand. "I mean it," she said.

First confusion, then rejection flitted across his face. He slumped down on the couch, making it creak loudly. She heard the tea splash into his glass, but he didn't drink what he had poured. He rearranged the few candies left on the plate.

"I'm going to call Antonio's house," she said, crossing to the little table with the phone on it. Turning her back to him so he wouldn't see her disturbed state, she thumbed through the phone book with trembling fingers. The pages wouldn't turn fast enough. She couldn't quite remember how Antonio spelled his last name. The silence around her added to her acute discomfort.

She dialed Antonio's house. After about thirty rings she hung up.

"He's not home," she said.

"Come and sit down. You look pale," Josh said.

She sat down self-consciously. "We have to get out," she said. "Antonio has surely had enough time to get to the hospital. And he must have a manager the security service can call. There's usually more than one person listed to receive the calls."

"Do you really want to?"

Her heart hammered. Not trusting her eyes to meet his, she picked up the notebook in which she'd jotted down the numbers of the carpets they had decided to rent and flipped the page back to the number for the security company, thinking, *Distance is the only way to sanity.*

From the corner of her eye, she could see the disappointment on his face as he ran his fingers through his hair.

"You sure we've selected enough carpets? Shouldn't we be looking at a few more? I haven't even seen a goat-hair carpet yet," he said.

She chose to overlook the goat humor, which fell as flat as his voice. Deliberately she sought out her reliable business self.

"We've selected enough for now. Ginger and you can select the others." Hearing her own calm professional voice reassured her that she was back in control.

As she turned to dial, she felt his presence behind her. Close. Sensual. Tempting. Willing herself to get on with the task at hand, she finished dialing.

The security-company guard acted shocked and suspicious and began grilling her. "How did you get in? What do you mean you're locked in? I'm looking at the alarm panel here. Our guard is on the way."

At that moment a siren howled and three armed men burst into the room. Obviously the guard had kept her on the phone while he dispatched the others. One of the men talked into a portable phone. Then he turned around and smiled. "Everything's okay. The shop owner says you're legit and sends you his apologies. He said he'll call you tomorrow. We are to escort you out." The guard led them to the front door.

In the parking lot Josh walked Darcy to her car. The palm of his hand was on her back, burning an insistent request through the fabric of her dress.

They stood silently at her car door for a moment, unaware of anything but each other.

At last he said, "Let's go to dinner."

She shook her head. "Josh, I can't. I have plans with my family."

"I would be glad to see your parents again."

"Sorry, we have some business matters to discuss. I'll go to dinner with you, Ginger and Billy next week."

A nerve worked in his jaw, as though she had slapped him in the face. But self-protection weighed as heavily on her as finding the money to preserve her heritage in Phoenix.

6

DARCY SAT in her office the next day debating whether to call Antonio at home or at his shop to ask about his daughter, when *he* called *her*.

"By the grace of God, I have a healthy grandson. Dimitri and his mother are fine. There were some complications, but the doctors are good. Very good. I have one small request of you."

"Of course," Darcy replied, imagining it would be connected to the carpet rentals.

"In honor of the birth of Dimitri, I am requesting the two of you to dine at my brother-in-law's restaurant tonight. You will do this for me and make me grateful?"

Startled, she said, "The two of us?"

"You and Mr. Cartwright. You brought us good luck."

"Well, I don't know his schedule. I'm sure he has plans—" Darcy cut herself off and began again. "I'll be honored. I can't speak for Mr. Cartwright, but yes, I'll be glad to attend the celebration."

"I ran into Mr. Cartwright this morning in the coffee shop. He is pleased to attend," Antonio said. "My brother-in-law's restaurant is called the Olive Basket. On M street. My family and I look forward to your company."

Darcy had been about to ask for a rain check, but then realized that after opening his shop for her, Antonio would take it as a personal insult. Failing to go dine and toast his grandson when he'd trusted them with his entire shop would not be taken lightly by Antonio.

After work that evening as she drove on to M street, she felt unsure about two things, one of which was easier to solve than the other. The gift, for instance. She hadn't bought a baby gift and there wasn't time now, but she would have it sent. A cute outfit or a soft teddy bear. The second problem—Josh—was much harder to solve. He had called right after Antonio to suggest they go together, and she had vetoed that idea, drumming up an excuse.

Now, fatigued from the myriad little tugs that Josh had made at the wall around her heart, Darcy decided she would put in an appearance at the restaurant and then slip away.

JOSH REACHED the Olive Basket before Darcy and stood eagerly under the sign of oversize purple olives, blessing Antonio.

His shop, the birth of his grandson and this invitation to their family celebration had all drawn Darcy closer to him. Josh sighed. "You're slipping up, man," he muttered. Instead of kissing Darcy as she wanted him to, he'd leaned on her and held her, battling his desires, hoping she'd kiss him. What a wimp he was!

And she sure could play hard to get. Of all the women he'd ever known, Darcy was the most reserved. On a physical level she clearly wanted him, even if she didn't instigate or lead. But on some other level she had erected a wall against him. Or was it against all men? It most likely had to do with her being in love with George. That scumbag had certainly figured in Darcy's sensitive and complex personality. He wanted her to sort out her problems herself, before she decided *he* was the problem and tried to distance herself from him. Oh, how well he remembered waiting for her to return those calls. And he was determined to get her to find him indispensable, on her terms. This hesitation on his part just had to stop. He should quit worrying about scaring her off and getting rejected again.

Where was she, anyway? The minute Darcy got there, he could speak to her like Arnold Schwarzenegger. "Let's get out of here and go to bed," Josh said aloud with an Austrian accent and groaned. It sounded silly.

Her cool classy manner had made him notice her that time at the party so long ago. He thought again about how George had shooed him away and then jilted her.

Despite that, she'd turned cold eyes on him when he kissed her on her forehead that awful day. Well, he was holding back now, giving her time to adjust to her own feelings because he didn't want to lose her again. But it was too hard on him physically.

As soon as she came in, he decided, he would tell her that he needed her, wanted her. George was a mistake, and as best man, he should have taken charge and averted the disaster that had made her so gun-shy. He should have talked sense into George the night before the wedding when that bimbo had thrown herself into George's arms. Josh swore aloud.

"Sorry I'm late and have you swearing," she said. "But I must have hit every red light."

Checking her watch, she walked through the door he held open for her. Only five minutes late and Josh was irritated.

Greek music playing softly in the background immediately drew them into another world. The cavernous room was decorated with strategically placed pedestals that held enormous baskets arranged with broccoli, herbs, Boston lettuce and other edible greens, with bunches of dark luscious olives tucked prominently throughout.

A petite black-haired woman with gold earrings as big as pea pods emerged to greet them. "Ah, Mr. Cartwright," she said. "I'm Helena, Antonio's sister."

"And Dimitri's aunt," Josh added. "Congratulations from Darcy and me."

Following Helena past the pedestals, she was disturbed by Josh's closeness and wished she could just go home and curl up with a book. Since the carpet-store episode, his sense of humor and fun-loving ways were outweighing her basic assessment of him as a serious type.

She didn't realize she winced as she took her seat.

"You okay?" Josh asked.

"Oh, just my shoe. I'll slip it off." She smiled, but inwardly she struggled with that unexplainable urge consuming her to hold his hand, ask him to talk about himself.

Josh was commenting on the decor, noting how someone had gotten quite creative with the broccoli.

"I never would have thought broccoli could be attractive," he said.

"It's decorative," Darcy replied, "And tastes wonderful, too. I could eat broccoli three times a day."

"Boy, you're getting cantankerous," he said, and laughed. "So we don't like the same vegetables. It isn't a big deal."

It wasn't what he didn't like that upset her. It was what she knew she would like to have.

Darcy watched him start to speak, clear his throat and hesitate. She waited, sure he was going to talk about George and why he had run away. George was the only topic that could cause him to look so tense. Good. About time he discussed what had happened. If he didn't, she could never trust him, for it meant his loyalties lay with the man who had wronged her.

"Well, I don't know where to begin," he said, then hesitated again, averting his eyes. Darcy turned pale, wondering what she would say. Telling him she wasn't interested in why George hadn't shown up would be a blatant lie. She wanted to know the whole despicable truth. Spoken aloud.

"We've been avoiding talking about George. Tell me what..." She trailed off as she felt a hand on her shoulder.

"Fancy running into you here," said a familiar voice.

Darcy swung around. "Oh, Mother, this is nice. Hi, Dad." Delighted, she sprang from her chair, napkin flying off her lap, to embrace her parents.

"Antonio called. He urged us to come and celebrate his grandson's birth. 'A baby is a family festival,' Antonio said, and he wasn't kidding. He got you here, too. Hello, Josh."

Her father shook hands with Josh. Darcy could see Josh's presence spark instant pleasure on her parents' faces. They'd spoken so highly of him after that fateful day. Considerate, they'd called him. Worrying that they'd think she was dating Josh, Darcy set out to clarify the situation. Clearing her throat, she said, "We were selecting carpets for Josh's sister's wedding when Antonio had to leave."

Her mother nodded. "That's a good way to get to know each other. Selecting furnishings together, wallpapering together, sometimes even cooking together can tell a man and a woman if they're going to be happy."

Darcy's mouth fell open. *This is awful!*

Before she could protest, Josh said, "Your mother is absolutely right, Darcy. I've seen a lot of couples fight over shopping for things. We didn't have one argument over the carpets for Ginger's wedding. You have great taste and knowledge about oriental rugs. Now, of course, we haven't wallpapered or cooked together."

He had to be joking. But his eyes were serious as he said, "If Darcy and I cooked together, she would hate the way I either undercook or overcook."

Darcy crumpled her napkin, trying desperately to think of some way to bring the discussion around to something impersonal. But her mother was addressing Josh, recounting the time early in her marriage when she found out how her husband hated to have vegetables overcooked and she liked them barely steamed. "As time passed we each gave a little," her mother said.

As Darcy listened to her mother's dissertation on compromise in marriage, she waited impatiently for Josh to say something about Ginger. But he was nodding along, agreeing. Her father, much to her horror, was interjecting his own philosophical comments into the conversation.

Helena arrived and asked if they liked the table. "I can find you a booth if you wish."

"This is fine," Josh said. "You must tell us more about Greek food."

Helena smiled, her pea-pod earrings swinging as she nodded her head. "It will be my pleasure." The waiter had arrived carrying a tray loaded up with rice wrapped in grape leaves, moussaka, grilled eggplant in a succulent tangy sauce, souvlaki and other dishes. Helena explained them all.

As they began dining, Josh and her father started talking about the price of lumber, which was in itself surprising. She had no idea Josh knew a two-by-four from a tree trunk, but he held his own admirably before her dad, whose whole career revolved around his lumberyard. Her father went on to talk about how his father had taught him simple carpentry when he was a kid in Phoenix, and how much he enjoyed working with tools.

George had never been able to converse with her father about lumber or anything else and always ended up making her dad angry. "That self-important punk," her dad had called George once. Darcy quickly turned her attention to the spit-broiled lamb and away from

Josh. Good conversation was an art anyone could develop.

"This food is wonderful," her mother said, then added, "If you like Greek food, Josh, you should have Darcy cook for you. She does wonders with phyllo dough."

"I'm hoping," he said, looking at Darcy in a way that made her heart pound.

Her parents, much to her distress, were behaving as though she and Josh were an item. Cora signaled her daughter. "Excuse us," she said, rising and leading Darcy to the ladies' room.

"You're sitting there like a bump on a log, Darcy. Josh is an extremely eligible bachelor, and there's no question of his interest in you. I'd say the man's in love with you. He has a special way of looking at you. Plus, he's handsome, charming and has the manners of a prince. He's intelligent and considerate and polite."

Darcy washed her hands and turned off the faucet, wondering where to start. Her mother did want the best for her.

"I'm planning his sister's wedding. And, Mother, this is another one of those times I wished I had a sister or a brother so you wouldn't bug me. I'm not going to get serious about anyone and provide you with grandchildren. You have to accept that."

"I don't think you should let him get away. He's giving you every opportunity to express your interest."

"Mother," Darcy protested. "Antonio trapped us into this, not that I'm not glad about his grandson. But you and Dad are embarrassing me, talking about marriage and compromise. A rich man like Josh will think you like his money, so let's please keep it impersonal."

"Think about what I'm saying. Your father and I don't care how rich he is. He's a good man. Decent. Don't act so stubborn. Just do one thing for me. Don't back away from Josh if he expresses an interest in you, and he *is* doing that. In a big way."

Leaving the ladies' room, Darcy wondered how her mother could read so much into Josh's words or manner. He hadn't made one attempt tonight to flirt with her. He was not her date.

Yet she blushed as he rose when she and Cora returned to the table. She wasn't sure if it had to do with her mother's confident appraisal of him or the way he was looking at her.

As his gaze tangled warmth around her soul, her heart began to flutter. And for a wild second she thought it was pounding a tune. But the band had set up and was playing a foreign tune that reminded her of strong winds blowing through narrow treetops. The sounds were wild and free, and the beat of drums announced impending action. About to ask Josh if he thought a floor show would follow, Darcy was startled by the arrival of the maître d'.

"I'm Armand, Antonio's chief feaster," he said. "I request you join me in the celebration." He took Darcy's hand in his and urged her out of her seat. "Come on, sir," he said to Josh. "I want you to join your lady. And I'd like the two of you—" he addressed her parents "—to come and dance with us as well. Dimitri's birth brings us all joy."

As Armand led Darcy away, she could see another feaster rounding up the other guests.

"Hold her this way," Armand told Josh, and he demonstrated by putting both hands on Darcy's waist from behind, swaying from the right to left.

Josh grinned. "Thank you," he said, and Armand winked at him. The warmth of Josh's hands, tightly possessive around her waist, spun excitement through her.

Another waiter had begun to line up the other diners behind them in a flutter of expectation.

Just as Josh's hands were pulling her closer to him, Armand stepped in front of her. Placing Darcy's hands on his own waist, Armand led the line of dancers around the dining room till all the diners, at least seventy-five of them, had joined in the dancing.

Josh's hands were moving, slowly at first, then sliding upward. As she swayed, the movement involuntarily shook her taut breasts into his hands. The soft fabric caressing in a circular movement made her pant, and a deep tremor ran through her to his hands.

As Armand moved faster, leading her on, Josh's hands slipped lower and jostled her closer, and she moved with gusto, following Armand, who led the conga line out into the street. Pedestrians stopped to gawk and listen to the lively music pouring out of the restaurant.

They danced up the street, turned around and danced back into the restaurant, circling the room. Armand started doing a peppy two steps to the right, two steps to the left, clapping enthusiastically. And the rest followed. Darcy began laughing and the other dancers started whistling and clapping. She was glad the tempo had picked up and Josh had let go of her waist, but at the same time, she had been enjoying his touch.

The band shifted to a slow number. Armand took Darcy's hands and joined them with Josh's. "The couple of the evening," he yelled, "will lead in a waltz."

Josh laughed, drew Darcy into his arms and led her onto the dance floor even as she protested. As they swayed to the music, he drew her closer till his cheek touched hers. "I knew I should have taken ballroom-dancing lessons," he said as he stepped on her toe.

"We're doing fine," she said. "Just don't try to dip me."

"Is dipping part of the waltz?" he asked, doing what she'd asked him not to do, making her hair fly back. He towered over her, gazing down mischievously.

When he pulled her back up, she said, "That dip wasn't as good as almond mocha, but it was okay."

He groaned. "You led me into it. Is this your standard line for a dancing partner?"

"Yeah," she said. "Every Tuesday night I go waltzing, and every Thursday night I have cha-cha lessons, and—"

"You like dancing that much?" He held her away, then laughed when he saw her grin.

Others were beginning to dance, and Darcy was relieved the attention was off them. The music changed to a twist.

Darcy said, "Now this is one dance I haven't mastered. Let's go sit."

At the table her mother half rose. "Come do the twist with me, Ralph."

"If I hadn't danced in the streets, I would," Ralph wheezed, mopping his brow. His wife slumped back into her chair.

"Will you dance with me?" Josh asked, and Cora got to her feet with a big smile.

"How nice of you," she said, bursting with pleasure.

Darcy watched. Not having had a son, both her parents had always made a joke of saying how they could hardly wait to have a son-in-law. They'd seemed hesitant around George, though; it was obvious they had reservations about him. When she'd pressed, all they'd said was that they were looking forward to getting to know him better. After the debacle at the altar, they had quit spinning their son-in-law fantasy—at least they had until tonight.

As Josh led her mother onto the dance floor, Darcy said to her dad, "I'm exhausted and my feet are killing me. These shoes are awful. Would you please tell Mother and Josh that I had to leave? I'll call him tomorrow about the dog. See if he found the owner."

Her father wheezed, coughed, then asked, "What dog?"

"Long story about a stray. Josh can fill you in." She rose and kissed her father on his cheek. "I'll call Mother tomorrow morning." Stopping to thank Antonio and congratulate him again, she ran to her car. Her dad's asthma was certainly getting worse. She'd been able to hear his coughing above the music, and the music was loud. Phoenix would be such a good escape for all of them.

7

LATE THAT NIGHT, the phone rang, and sure it was Josh, Darcy ran to pick it up. It was a wrong number. When it rang again, it was her mother. "I can't believe you sneaked out like that," she said. "We were all having such a good time. Josh said he had fun."

"He's good at making people feel important, always says the right things," Darcy replied. She'd thought her mother would have waited till the next day to rehash the evening. And much as she loved her mother, she wasn't in any mood to talk about Josh.

"And what's wrong with that? You could try doing some of that yourself, dear. He looked crestfallen when your dad said you'd left. For a minute I thought he was going to run after you. Then he sat down and started talking about fishing and picnics."

She liked that description of him. Crestfallen. But her mother, ever wishing and hoping, could have imagined it. "Josh likes to fish?" Darcy chuckled. "I suppose he talked about the big one that got away."

"He was talking about all the things he never got to do as a child because he never knew his real father and the two stepfathers were older men who had already raised their sons and didn't want to mess around with another. So Josh fished in the stream. Alone."

"How come he was talking so much about himself? It's strange for a grown man to do that with people he doesn't really know," she said.

"Your dad was talking about going fishing in Canada or Florida, and Josh got so envious. Before the evening was up, the two were making plans to go deep-sea fishing in Florida this winter."

"How nice," Darcy said. Josh was moving in on her family. Soon he'd be visiting Great-Uncle Albert with them and taking flowers to her grandmother's grave, singing Christmas carols and decorating Aunt June's Christmas tree with the rest of them. As vivid pictures of her family's traditions filled her mind, she was both resentful and pleased. She hadn't voted on Josh's adoption, but she supposed he could be a family friend.

"He wanted to know if you and I would go. And I told him I was sure of it, considering how much you like to fish."

"I plan to go to Jamaica this winter with Amy from the office. I'll take one week of vacation then and take the other week this fall to go out West," Darcy said, hurriedly trying to set the record straight. "And, Mother, you know I never liked fishing. I hate putting the bait on. Yuck."

Her mother sidestepped. "Why would you want to go on vacation with Amy when you could go with a handsome guy like Josh? I don't understand you, dear." Cora sighed. "Anyway, it's getting late. I plan to sleep in tomorrow morning, so don't phone me, phone Josh. He said he'd be waiting for your call. There's something about that dog he wants to discuss with you."

After hanging up, Darcy scrubbed the kitchen floor. It was easier not to think when you were enveloped in ammonia fumes. Already she'd felt Josh's presence in the laundry room. A dryer, she knew, would never be just a dryer again for her. And lying in bed, was a sure way to bring on thoughts of his touch, his kiss, his stirring gaze.

She vacuumed the living room and then the bedroom, filling her mind with the loud whirr of machinery. Finally, exhausted, she fell into bed, where there were soft clean sheets and an emptiness she couldn't chase away.

The next morning she showered and, moving lethargically, carried her coffee to the phone and sat sipping, wishing she hadn't said she'd call but wondering what was going on with the dog. "Well, you're a big boy, Josh, you can handle it," she said to the phone. Then she got to her feet, deciding to go for a walk.

It was eight o'clock and the streets were quiet. A few joggers were out, headbands soaked with sweat and tanned bodies dripping wet. In just a couple of hours the crowds would start arriving from the suburbs to stroll the cobblestoned streets and window-shop. There was everything from trendy boutiques to second-hand shops.

Fred's Flowers had just opened for the day, and Darcy paused, smelling the spicy carnations and snapdragons. She began sneezing and knew, before she looked, the cause for it. Tucked in were red roses, and their cloying fragrance tended to stick to her brain like a bad memory. Wheezing, she moved away from the roses and reset her brain to the present.

Snapdragons were Uncle Albert's favorite flowers, and no matter how he pretended to hate all flowers now, she would drop some off for him. She also remembered that flowers had to be ordered for the Whalen party that Dreams, Inc., was catering next week. Aunt June had expressed dissatisfaction with Fancy Flowers, despite two years of working with them. New owners and poor fast-fading stock had just about taken the bloom off the last event. So, Aunt June wouldn't object to her giving this neighborhood shop a chance to supply flowers. She stood waiting for the shopkeeper to finish setting up his displays for the day.

The minute he heard her request—for the snapdragons and the Whalen order—the owner beamed. "Step into my office," he said.

The "office" was a desk in the back of the shop next to the glassed-in refrigerators, which held bright exotic flowers. He pointed to a chair for Darcy, and then she described what she wanted for the Whalen party. "I don't see many wildflowers in your shop here, so I don't know if you can supply—"

"For you, honey, I'll go pick the wildflowers myself." Fred smiled. "Let me pull out the list of seasonal flowers and prices." He swiveled around to a steel filing cabinet behind his desk.

She leaned back in her chair, enjoying the fresh fragrance of the shop, and glanced casually at the stack of papers on his desk. A clipboard sat atop with a list of the day's orders. "Priority Customers," read the heading, and she proceeded to scan the names below. "Cartwright, Josh." She did a double take, twisting her watch band. Next to his name was a list of women's names.

"Somebody you know?" Fred asked.

She tapped Josh's name with her fingernail.

"Good customer. Now, he'll give us a good reference if you need one," Fred raved. "He's got a bunch of women he sends flowers to every month. Don't know how he keeps 'em all on the string—I oughtta take lessons from him. But I don't mean to gossip. The point I'm making is that our flowers keep them coming. Ha, ha."

Darcy blanched, but it wasn't because of the hefty bid the shopkeeper had just handed her for the Whalen wildflowers. As payment for the snapdragons, she endorsed and handed him the one blank check she carried on her walks. Vaguely aware of having bought at least eight bunches more than she wanted, she stood to leave.

"We could deliver these this afternoon, and we'd love to do the wildflowers for you," Fred said. "By the way, your watch is hanging on your wrist."

She peeled the watch off, amazed at having twisted the beat-up leather band to a shred. Pocketing it, she said, "I'll call you about the wildflowers." She extended her arms for him to load the flowers. "I live just two blocks away. I think I can make it."

As she walked along, inhaling the spicy scent of the crimson, yellow and white snapdragons, all she could think of was Josh. Underneath all that charm he poured on her, he was no different from his old friend George. Josh was adept at playing the numbers, sending flowers to different women, while making each one think she was special. Well, she could buy her own flowers. As many as she wanted, even if she had to skip lunch for a month. And Josh could go to hell. How could she *ever* have let the fact that Josh and George were one of a kind slip her mind?

Apparently Josh was dedicated to developing his technique of lovemaking. And if she could see straight, through the cloud of anger she felt toward George, she had to admit he hadn't really run around with a bunch of women. He had merely left her, publicly, for the girlfriend he'd somehow kept a secret. After hours and hours of self-flagellation about how she'd failed George in and out of bed, she had concluded that George had been going with that woman forever. Still, she couldn't help but think that the other woman had manipulated George, who wasn't basically a bad person. She shook her head, trying to dispel her confusion and hurt.

Steaming at the deceptiveness of men, Darcy stumbled to her door and started juggling the snapdragons, wildly trying to retrieve the keys from her pocket.

"Here, let me help you," said a familiar male voice.

She jumped. "What're you doing here?"

Josh took the flowers from her in one easy scoop. "Looks like you're getting ready for a major party," he said.

She thought she heard accusation and almost decided to let him think she was throwing a bash to which he wasn't invited. But such games took too much energy, and she wasn't in the habit of playing them. Finding her keys, she unlocked the door and held it open for him. "In the kitchen, please," she said.

As he piled the snapdragons on the counter, leaves and petals scattered over the gleaming floor. She began picking them up hurriedly and tossing them down the garbage disposal. "I have to find a vase," she said, opening and shutting the cupboard doors. Finding one tall and one small vase, she set those on the counter and sighed, frustrated.

"Here," Josh said, putting the stopper in the sink and turning on the faucet. "This'll keep them fresh till you start arranging them. They smell wonderful."

Darcy shot him an appreciative glance. He was so good at doing all the little things that needed to be done. Well practiced at winning a woman's heart, this same guy would run away if a woman got too close to him. Wasn't that usually why men dated different women at the same time? She flipped on the garbage disposal and let that noise add to the angry tremor filling her. She took the watch from her pocket and slapped it down on the counter.

"You don't look very happy," Josh said. "What's wrong? How did you break your watch band?"

He put his arms around her.

There was real comfort and strength in his arms, his troubled eyes, his soft voice. He projected safety and genuine caring, and she leaned into all those feelings like an exhausted swimmer clinging to a dock.

"Nothing's wrong. I just went to Fred's Flowers. You know where that is? You're familiar with it."

Puzzled at the heat in her voice, he stared. "Yes, I am. I'd have to be blind not to notice Fred's Flowers—I drive by the shop twice a day."

Don't add me to your list of girlfriends.

"You didn't buy all these flowers, did you, Darcy? Are they for a Dreams, Inc., function?"

"I wanted to buy the flowers," she said, setting her chin firmly, carefully omitting Great-Uncle Albert from the scenario. "I like buying my own flowers."

He laughed. "That's not like the women I know."

Triumph rang out in his voice and solidified what she'd heard about him. He was proud of his list. She swept up the crimson snapdragons and thrust them in the tall white vase she'd filled with water. Fluffing out the bouquet, she carried it into the living room.

"Looks nice," he said, following her.

"What brings you here, Josh? Any word about the dog's owners?" she asked, refluffing the bouquet until all the stalks fanned out evenly.

"No," he said, sinking into a chair. "In fact, he's in the Jeep. Locked up and waiting. I thought you might want to take a ride out with me to the Humane Society. My building super is on my case and I have to do something." He looked resigned.

"You're not going to turn him in, are you? The *dog pound?*"

"Don't look at me that way. It's not something I want to do. But I'm running out of options and time. I called several of my co-workers and even tried to give him to your parents last night, but they say they're not interested. The old cats would have a fit."

"They would. Mitzi is twelve and Rambo is fifteen. And they're so set in their ways and spoiled they start taking revenge, like peeing in the bathtub, if something doesn't go their way. They have their lives in order."

He sighed. "Wish I did."

Noting the tired droop to his eyes and voice and shoulders, Darcy was sure he was going to elaborate.

"So I thought you'd like to say goodbye to the dog," he said, standing up. "Coming?"

"We can't turn Bumpers in. If no one claims him within forty-eight hours they'll put him to sleep. That's their standard procedure." She protested so loudly he sat down.

"Bumpers? Is that what you're calling him?" He grinned.

She smiled. "I just thought of it—he did bump into us, I mean, the Jeep. Can't you bribe your super to let you keep him a few more days? We'll run an ad. I'll spring for it and we'll make posters. I can do that on my computer at work and tack them to trees all over Georgetown."

"My super couldn't be bought. Maybe yours can," he said hopefully. "Any chance you can take Bumpers for a few days?"

Darcy wavered. The dog's cute pleading face sprang to her mind, but she knew her building was strict. They only allowed birds. No children. No dogs or cats.

"I see you're debating. Bumpers will be grateful to you forever, and it'll at least buy him some time. Maybe his distraught owners will see the posters or the ad and call."

Bumpers had managed to claim her friendship as no dog had. She couldn't let him down. "Okay, he can move in with me till we get caught."

Josh reached for her and hugged her. "You're a kind and generous woman," he said. "I'll go get him."

"Wait. We have to sneak him in after dark. I ran into the super this morning, and he said he's going to do some fixing up today. We don't want to run into him. But we can't just leave Bumpers in the Jeep."

He glanced at his watch. "We could take him for a drive and get some burgers."

"It's only one o'clock and it doesn't get dark till eight. Are we going to drive to New York City?"

"We could. Take in a play. Go to Coney Island." He grinned again. "Anything is possible with us."

There was no mistaking the intent in his eyes, and Darcy's heart beat wildly. He moved closer and gently lifted her chin. "Anything is possible with us," he repeated, gazing into her eyes. "When you're ready, let me know. I'll be waiting."

She moved away, afraid of melting and pleading for him to kiss her.

In the kitchen she shook her head silently, cursing that intangible thing called sex appeal. He had more of it than any man had a right to, and all those women who got flowers from him knew it. Was he different to each one, or did he apply the same masterly techniques? When she was an old woman, she'd probably look back at this time in her life and wish she'd taken Josh up on all his unspoken but deeply conveyed propositions. Her eye fell on the flowers heaped in the sink.

"They really brighten up your kitchen," Josh said from behind her.

"They could just as well brighten up the lives of those who can't garden anymore," she said. "I just got an idea—why don't we drop them all off at the Dumbar-

ton Nursing Home? Uncle Albert will have his snapdragons and so will all his friends."

"Darcy, you're full of surprises, always thinking of
the most practical way to do something for somebody
else."

It was her turn to be surprised. She couldn't think of
what she'd done for anyone lately. "Flowers are practical?" she asked, hoping the hostility that gripped her
concerning his list was well hidden.

"In certain circumstances, yes," he said, picking the
armload of snapdragons out of the sink, shaking the
water off of them and wrapping the stems in paper
towels.

She bit her tongue. Flowers were doubtless his practical way to tell a woman, *See ya baby, last night was
great, but I'm on to my next conquest.*

When they got to the car, Bumpers was beside himself with joy at seeing her. He jumped into her arms
yelping and licking her face. Pleased at the reception,
she tried to calm him down, stroking his scruffy little
head.

Josh set the flowers on the back seat of the Jeep before getting in. "Good news, Bumpers—you'll get to
sleep with Darcy tonight," he said in a tight voice.

Glad Uncle Albert's nursing home was only around
the corner, she held the dog close, and he turned grateful eyes up to her. Silently she promised him he wasn't
going to the pound.

The receptionist at the nursing home informed them
that Uncle Albert was in physical therapy, then bingo,

but she would put the snapdragons Darcy had set aside for him in his room.

"And I'll set these others in the dining room and the bingo hall," the efficient lady said, flashing them an appreciative smile.

Back in the Jeep, Josh asked, "Would you like to see my office?"

She nodded, curious. He drove down to Pennsylvania Avenue and parked the Jeep in front of a concrete-and-glass mid-rise, two blocks from the White House.

"We're taking Bumpers in? Won't that cause a problem?"

"Not when I own the business," he said. "Besides, it's Sunday."

The spacious lobby had a huge glass-domed ceiling, drawing in the sun and sky to the jungle flourishing below. He'd bought a red collar and leash for Bumpers, who was walking gingerly, skipping and halting across the highly polished marble floors. They laughed and quickly led him onto the elevator. Josh pressed the button for the penthouse.

Once there, he punched his code into a wall panel. "The security here is really tight. Pose with me," he said. He pulled her in his arms, hugged her, then released her. "We're now photographed, the doors are unlocked and they'll lock behind us, just like at the carpet place." He touched her cheek with the back of his hand and she moved away.

He led her down a narrow white carpeted hallway into his office. It was huge with sleek gray and white modern furniture and gleaming chrome-and-glass tables and lamps.

"Have a seat. I have to sign a few papers and pick up the prenuptial agreements my lawyer has drawn up for Billy," he said, sitting down behind the desk.

It didn't surprise her that Josh was taking steps to protect his sister, but surely he was overly concerned. Bumpers plopped down on the white carpet and promptly went to sleep.

She sat on a chair by the desk, idly studying the abstract paintings on the wall, trying to avoid staring at their handsome owner. But frequently her eyes traveled fondly to him, anyway. He looked dead serious reading what she assumed was the agreement for Billy.

"If you have work to do, I'll take Bumpers to La-Fayette Park for a walk," she offered.

"This'll only take a minute. You're not looking to get mugged, are you?" His eyes twinkled. "Did you bring your watch along?" Seeing her nod, he said, "We'll stop and buy a new band for it. You're not bored, are you?"

She shook her head. *Bored with you?* Since getting locked up with him in the carpet shop, her mind had been spinning endless fantasies of exploring Josh. His intelligence and vigor made him interesting. His considerate ways, his ability to converse with people of all ages, his kindness to the dog, his concern for his sister were all qualities that won her heart. But the thought of that list made her stomach churn. How many of those women on the list had he brought here on a Sunday to stretch out with him on these white carpets? She sat stiffly, trying to put Josh from her mind.

But his presence created a compelling eagerness in her for his touch. His dark hair, the way he held his pen, his confident authoritative way of signing a memo held her total attention. Deep inside her, an uprising pounded on the wall around her heart, clamoring for him. She wanted to press her lips against his face and have him dip her again as he had on the dance floor, but this time she wanted to do more than waltz. Maybe it was inevitable.

He glanced up and smiled, and her heart beat faster. "I'm feeling tired, I guess," she murmured, wondering at her attempt at explaining her inner turmoil.

"We could rent a hotel room, since we can't take Bumpers anywhere till dark, then we could *both* take a nap." He chuckled. "Or—" he stretched his arms over his head, so handsome, sexy, graceful "—we could stretch out right here."

"I've been invited to a hotel room before, but never with a canine chaperon," she said, trying to keep things light.

He laughed and came around the desk. Standing behind her, he massaged her neck and shoulders. His hands moved down, circling rhythmically over her back, soothing away one type of tension and spreading another. She closed her eyes and leaned against his chest, breathing in his divine male scent. Then, squirming out of his grasp and grabbing onto sanity, she rose from her chair. "Did the massage help?" he asked in a ragged voice.

Help? The warm tenderness his hands had imprinted on her through the fabric were melting her resolve, lighting a fire that was going out of control. "Yes. I'll take Bumpers for a walk," she sighed.

"But first," he said and gulped, gazing at her, "I want to show you something."

8

CURIOSITY AND DESIRE nibbled at her. What was he going to show her? Watching him walk to his desk, so tall and strong, she felt her heart miss a beat and wild images hurtled through her mind. His kissing technique? She gulped. He pulled open a desk drawer and removed a wood-framed photograph. Her heart sank. He was going to show her a picture of the woman he loved, the reason he'd never married.

"This is the only existing photograph of my father and me," Josh said, handing it to her.

The black-and-white photograph within the polished frame was battered on the edges and discolored by water spots. A tall handsome dark-haired man stood with his arm around a solemn boy—a boy who'd grown into the strapping man beside her. She saw his resemblance to his father. Same straight nose and square face and dark eyebrows.

"How old were you when this was taken?" she asked.

"Twelve. It was the day before my father took off for good, not that he was around much before that," Josh said sadly. "For years I believed it was my fault. Ginger was only a baby then."

Pain hollowed his eyes and saddened her. How could a man abandon his son? Seeing the hurt and anger cross his face, a great wave of tenderness filled her. An image of Josh clasping the photo at night against his teary face tugged at her heart.

"Your dad would be proud of you if he saw you today, Josh. You're kind and considerate and successful," she said softly, setting the picture on his desk.

"Think so?"

His eagerness to believe her words clutched at her heart. She smiled and nodded. Then she reached up and touched his face, tracing a finger across his cheekbone, wishing she could erase the hurt in his eyes.

In the next second all movement blurred. She reached out to hug him, and he embraced her tenderly. Her arms around his waist, she closed her eyes. His lips grazed her hair and his arms tightened, pulling her closer as he groaned her name and kissed her forehead. Compassion for him made her want to sweep away his shadows and comfort him as he'd never been comforted before. She brought one hand up to touch his face.

He reveled in it, closed his eyes and sighed. Then he traced his finger lightly across her lips and, feeling her assent, bent down to kiss her softly, lightly, before pressing passion. As she returned his kiss, she felt it so right, so overdue, so erotic. She sprinkled small kisses across his face, welcoming his deeper explorations. His hands moved slowly downward. So strong, so gentle.

"Darcy, I want you," he whispered roughly.

All protests fled her mind. He wanted her as much as she wanted him, and his fingers and words were building an expectation that was impossible to deny. Still, she tried. "We have to stop," she said in a barely audible voice.

"Do you really want to?" he asked, tracing her collarbone with his lips. Then he whispered, "One more kiss and I'll let you decide."

She knew she was lost to his smooth persuasion even before he kissed her.

"I want to undress you," he whispered. I want to worship you with my eyes. I want to look at these." He rubbed the palms of his hands across her breasts with slow steady insistence.

She buried her head on his broad shoulder, the crisp cotton of his shirt grazing her face, and the urge to discover his hidden pleasures made her breathe harder.

Undoing the top button of her shirt, slipping his hand in, he pulled her bra strap gently and spread hot little puffs of his ragged breath into the dip between her breasts. Grazing his face urgently with her hand, she started to undo the second button, but his hand closed over hers, stopping her.

He moved away and pulled her to her feet, then clasped her to him, caressing her back in wide circles, making her wild with anticipation.

"We can't go on," he said, and she stiffened.

"Why not?" she asked, her lower lip trembling, her heart sinking.

"Because Bumpers is watching," he said, hardly able to contain his laughter.

She laughed hysterically, pointing to the dog, who stood staring at them, eyes puzzled. At last, wiping her eyes on her sleeve, she said, "Thank you, Bumpers. You stopped me from doing something silly."

"You call this silly?" he asked, grabbing her again and kissing her with such passion that she clung to him, drew him closer and began expressing her own desire to taste his lips. Softly and gently at first, he kissed the corners of her full mouth, and she responded with all her heart, convinced it wasn't loneliness drawing her to him. Then slipping his tongue in, he made naughty little passes on the inside of her lips, fueling her passion. As he did that, he pulled her closer against him, fitting her between his thighs and loving her with his eyes, ah, such dreamy eyes.

Hair rumpled, breath ragged, he held her at arm's length, gazing at her like a man admiring a valuable painting. She blushed joyfully, and feeling magnificently female, she touched his face, ruffled his hair.

He knelt before her and unzipped her jeans. She heard the zipper, felt his breath and then his steady touch, pushing the denim down; she clutched at his hair. He rubbed her calves, kissed her knees, traced circles around her ankles, before standing up and kissing her lightly on the lips, fingers steadily unbuttoning her blouse.

When he stooped to kiss her stomach with a short tender press that melted through her, again she tugged at his hair, wanting him desperately. He was savoring every touch, stroking her tingling skin with quiet adoration.

He reached for the black lace of her briefs with his teeth, gently tugging at it, slipping his tongue behind it so briefly she thrust herself forward with a little cry. Front and back, his hands were setting her on fire as he pulled away the sheer panties and she stepped out of them so gracefully he moaned. Now he was kneeling again, just looking, and his worshipful eyes made her feel beautiful, shapely, admired, desired, needed. And sexy. Very sexy.

Agile as a panther, he sprang up and thumbed the fabric at her shoulders, conveying his unspoken need. He pulled off her shirt. Then he feasted his eyes before tenderly touching her breasts.

"We'll take it slow and easy," he said.

His ragged breath told her he was trying to convince himself to go slow and easy, even as his thumbs traveled beneath the lace, heightening the turmoil he was creating in her body. She reached behind her to unhook her bra.

"Let me undress you," he whispered, turning her around and kissing her back as he got rid of the lacy barrier.

"You're gorgeous," he said, turning her around, touching her cheekbone, making her quiver and reach for his belt buckle. "Slow is not easy." He sighed and drew an answering sigh from her.

An understatement if ever she had heard one. She closed her eyes and he kissed her until she gasped. Such passion. Such texture. And that smell of his after-shave tantalized her until she couldn't help nuzzling his neck, then moving steadily downward, tracing his skin with her lips.

He was moving faster, but not fast enough for her. Even while she understood on a subliminal level her need to be cherished, she wanted more. Now.

He undressed with expediency and fluidity, and before she could capture his muscular build with her eyes, he was pulling her closer. She felt his lips working magic on her breasts, making her moan. Then he lowered her to the floor, eased his body over hers and fit into her so naturally she gasped, tightening herself around him. He moved slowly, with an exquisite rhythm, putting infinite value on her pleasure, cherishing her with his every touch. Her response rocked her beyond belief, and he joined her in her ecstasy.

SHE WOKE UP in his arms, with Bumpers sprawled a foot away. She lay watching Josh sleep, a lock of hair tumbling forward on his brow, and a great emotion filled her just as Josh had filled her, and she knew it wasn't her imagination. She loved him. Or did she?

As soon as the word "love" crossed her mind, she rose and dressed rapidly, turning away from those long hard legs, that strong lean muscular body and those eyelashes, so lush and dark against his cheeks. How did this ever happen? How could she have gone this far? She'd leave a note, take a cab home. Nervousness turned her fingers into thumbs as she tried to button her shirt. When she was finally pulled together, she reached for her tennis shoes.

"You're something else," he said. "Come here."

"I really should get going," she said, blushing at his obvious readiness to make love to her again.

He jumped up, pulled on his underwear and said, "Wait. What's wrong? Weren't you . . . ?"

"It was perfect." She sighed. "We had great sex." *Love is too frightening, too definite.* She had doubled her vulnerability. The cocoon wouldn't help now.

"Is that all it was for you?" he asked, tucking in his shirt. "I know how much you enjoyed it."

Why had she even thought for one single second that she was in love with him? There was no way on earth she could be in love. Scars as thick as castle walls surrounded her heart, and with good reason. He stood humming something lighthearted while buttoning his shirt.

As they left the building, he put his arm around her and said, "Your parents are nice people. I had fun with them the other night. Your dad said he'd like to go fishing, and I would love to have you go with us, provided, of course, you don't catch the biggest fish." He hugged her to his side.

Enthusiasm brightened his eyes, and his closeness, his affectionate squeeze, the hot intimacy they'd just shared, were beginning to put little cracks in that defensive wall around her heart. And it worried her.

"Not catch the biggest fish? You've got to be kidding," she said.

They put Bumpers in the Jeep, and Josh held her hand, stroking her fingers. She found herself reflecting fondly on their afternoon. He drove her to a jeweler's, and after selecting an expensive leather watch band, he reached into his pocket.

"Thanks, but I'm paying," she said, groping in her purse and retrieving her wallet. He argued, but she would have none of it. When the salesman went to the cash register to ring up her payment, she gave Josh a sidelong glance and said softly, "I won't be a kept woman."

His eyes twinkled. "Too bad," he teased, "because I was thinking of setting you up in an apartment and buying you a Rolls and hiring a chauffeur."

"Sounds good, especially if the chauffeur is handsome and ten years younger than me." She chuckled.

The laughter in his eyes faded. "You like younger men? Is that what you're waiting for, a young punk?"

"A punk could be entertaining." She walked out the door he held open for her. "A serious punk would be even better. You know the kind who's on top of every fad that comes along. Paper clips through the nose. Tires around the neck, false teeth hanging from his ears."

He laughed. "You've really done a lot of heavy thinking about this," he said, climbing into the Jeep. "An old man like me doesn't stand a chance with you."

She smiled, thinking he was joking, but his body language told her otherwise. There was a sincerity there that touched her. She reached out and held his hand, and he relaxed a bit.

"Would you like a bite to eat?" he asked, and she nodded, realizing she was starved.

"Burgers," she said, thinking that he'd satisfied her other hunger gloriously. "If we go to a drive-in, Bumpers can stay with us."

They ate in the parking lot, letting Bumpers eat in the back seat off the paper sacks their food came in. Josh rattled the ice cubes in his empty cup like a kid, and she outrattled him with hers. Bumpers was clamoring for more, giving little barks and trying to climb into the front seat.

"Calm down," Darcy commanded the animal. "You have to be very quiet when I sneak you in."

"I'll wrap him in newspapers and carry him in. Then just before we go to bed, I'll sneak him back out and walk him."

It didn't sink in right away. He was planning to spend the night with her. The thought pleased her and she smiled shyly, blotting a tiny bit of mustard off her seat belt.

He turned onto Wisconsin Avenue, which was bustling with tourists. Inching along in the heavy traffic, he pointed to the crimson-and-white snapdragons. "Pretty flowers," he said, and she shuddered, imagining all those women getting flowers from Josh, sitting in their homes, overjoyed by his thoughtfulness. Hurt slammed into her. This man didn't stop with giving a woman the steamiest sex she ever dreamed of. He followed through with a flowery flourish. She fiddled with her seat belt, disturbed, angry at herself for having given in to her physical urges.

She should have had more sense than to trust her most secret self with Josh Cartwright, the practiced lover of countless women. How could she have opened herself up to the hurt that would surely follow? Just as it had before. But George's lovemaking hardly compared to what she'd just experienced with Josh. Still, she had to put the brakes on.

At that moment a police car came screeching up behind them, sirens filling the air. Two cops jumped out and began chasing a man wearing a baseball cap.

"Georgetown's changed," Josh said. "People have changed." He sighed. "So much crime. It's not safe to walk around anymore. You should be careful."

She twisted in her seat and saw the cops had pinned the man down on the pavement next to the florist's shop.

"It is amazing how Georgetown draws crime," she said. "And to think we're only ten minutes from the White House. One would think the president would do something about it."

"He is doing something about it. Blowing hot air. Talking tough."

Darcy and he went on to talk affectionately about Washington, D.C., each listing their reasons for living there. Eventually she said, "We love D.C. for the same things—the history, beautiful monuments, big old trees, embassy row, all the bridges. The fact that our city is a world center."

They turned a corner. "We're almost home, Bumpers. And what do you know, there's even a parking spot," Josh said, parking between a Mercedes and a Chevy. "Darcy, if you grab the newspapers, I can disguise Bumpers as the *Washington Post*."

Undoing the seat belt and stretching behind to the back seat, she retrieved the papers and Bumpers in one scoop.

"Thanks, Josh. I can manage to sneak Bumpers in. I don't see the super around, and I have a ton of stuff to get done."

He leaned on the steering wheel. "Is that a roundabout way of saying you don't want me to come in?"

"Yes," she muttered.

"Then how are you going to manage to walk him? You can't be serious about going out into the streets alone after what we just saw." He was trying to reason his way in and looking awfully cute in the process. "Are you afraid I'm going to kiss you again?"

Her memory filled in the sexy details, the incredible fit, the erotic touch of his teeth at her waist, and she was torn. Besides, it would be easier to sneak Bumpers in with help.

Josh didn't wait for her response. He wrapped Bumpers in the newspapers, patting him, talking softly to him.

"Let's go before he gets over his shock and starts barking."

She ran in and opened her front door. Josh rushed in behind her, slamming the door shut with his foot. Bumpers started barking immediately, filling her small apartment with awful noise.

"In here. We've got to get him away from the front door," Darcy said, running on into her bedroom.

"We've got to get him a muzzle," Josh said. "For a little guy, he's got the loudest bark."

He set the dog on the floor and Bumpers ran wildly around the room. Darcy quickly picked up the first of two stacks of fresh laundry and set them in the basket in the closet. When she swung around to get the other sack, she saw Josh holding up a pair of her black lace bikini panties, fingering the lace.

She snatched them away. "Dirty old man," she scolded.

"I may be old, but I showered this morning," he said. "I could shower again and you could keep a close eye on me, scrub-a-dub to make sure I'm really clean. Is the shower in there?" he started towing her toward the bathroom.

Laughing, she whacked him with the panties.

"Stop, it's getting me too hot," he said. "No, wait, do it again, I'm beginning to like it." He raced after her.

"Weirdo," she gasped as he pinned her down on the bed. She laughed as they tumbled together. "This has to stop," she said. "We can't get involved." She had to put on the brakes. She couldn't get in any deeper.

He leaned on his elbow and propped his head in his hand. His eyes danced. "Come to me, baby," he said in an exaggerated foreign accent of some sort.

She laughed again. Suddenly a loud banging on the apartment door drew wild barking from Bumpers and shattered the moment. Darcy scrambled to her feet.

"I hope it's not the super. If it is, what am I going to do about the dog?" she asked.

"Wait a minute. I'll handle it. You just hang on to Bumpers and keep him quiet," Josh said, running his hand through his hair, squelching the unruly dark waves.

She grabbed his arm. "No. The super doesn't know you. I'll go." Straightening her shirt, she walked out.

As the pounding erupted again, she yelled, "Coming!"

The super, a thin-faced man who loved exercising his power stood at the door, toothpick dangling from his mouth.

"Mrs. Parrish next door reported hearing a dog bark. You know the building rules?" he demanded.

"I know the building rules, Mr. Simmons." She smiled. "I also know you can buy a tape of a menacing dog bark."

"What will they think of next?" Mr. Simmons threw his hands up in the air. "Before you know it, they'll make recordings of people having sex." He winked. "You know, all the noises."

She frowned. "What kind of crude comment is that? I can't believe you just said that. Goodbye, Mr. Simmons."

She slammed the door shut, heaved a sigh of relief and listened, holding her breath. Then hearing his footsteps recede, she relaxed.

Josh emerged from the bedroom, holding Bumpers with one hand and clamping his jaws together with the other. Smiling, he quickly stepped back in and she followed, closing the door behind her.

"You're something else," he said. "Didn't even have to lie. Has that guy ever made a pass at you?"

"If you consider crudeness a pass, maybe, but sometimes I wonder if he isn't a little slow. How can a building super never have heard of dog tapes? The other thing about him is that he's got a one-track mind. He'll now be listening for the tape, and as for Mrs. Parrish, she's an owner of this building and has clout."

Stroking Bumper's head, Josh said, "I'd better check my messages. Maybe someone's called about Bumpers."

She led him to the phone in the kitchen. "I have to fill you in on the tents for Ginger's wedding. And we need to talk about invitations and food and entertainment. Do you want a band? Or strolling musicians?"

Josh groaned. "Let's not get into all that now. I have confidence in you. Just go ahead and handle everything. Ginger may have ideas, but she's pretty young and inexperienced." Josh looked uneasy, as though the character of Billy remained unresolved. Josh added, "There's a bag of dog food in my Jeep. I'll get it as soon as I call my answering service."

"I'm not quite sure I can sell Mr. Simmons on the 'dog tape needs dog chow' idea." She grinned. "Wait, if you give me the keys, I'll run out with a duffel bag to carry it in."

Taking his keys and her own, she sauntered out, old canvas bag in hand, hoping Mr. Simmons had gone to a movie.

"Don't get mugged," he called after her, and she grinned again. It was so good to have somebody caring about her, watching out for her. . . .

If he wasn't serious about her, would he still show the same concern? she asked herself, then answered yes. Sadly, unfortunately, yes. He was a considerate man. A nice guy.

Back in her apartment, she held the bag up triumphantly, laughing at Josh holding Bumpers in his lap with his hand clamped around the dog's mouth. He shook his head.

"No message about this lost soul," he said. "Can you take him to work with you tomorrow?"

"I'll call Aunt June," she offered. She had put work as far out of her mind as Timbuktu. Which was unlike her. Work had been her life. Work would be her salvation.

Aunt June was hesitant till Darcy mentioned Josh. "You mean he's there with you now?" Her voice softened, "Well, he is a client, so if that's what'll keep him happy. But it's only for a day or two, I hope."

"Bumpers is going to work," Darcy announced, hanging up.

Talking about work had reminded Josh of his own business, and he sat writing notes to himself in the living room. Darcy smiled at the cozy little domestic scene they'd created. An illusion, she reminded herself. It was best not to get too comfortable in it. She'd managed alone so far and enjoyed her independence. A husband had no place in her life.

"Want a soft drink?" she asked, wondering what she was going to give him for dinner. Lamb chops? Chicken á la king?

"Not right now. I think I can sneak Bumpers out for his walk while everyone's busy with dinner," he said.

After he left, Darcy sat in the side chair she'd refinished and propped her feet up on the cherry coffee table. Wondering what he thought of her living room, she cast an appraising look around. The navy blue couches with white pillows were secondhand. The coffee table she'd bought at a garage sale. Compared to his apartment and office, her surroundings were modest. He didn't act as though he noticed anything different, though. He didn't behave like a spoiled rich man. But then, according to George and Josh's own flower list, he noticed little besides the female form.

Her stomach knotted. She was now on his damn list. He sent flowers to women he had sex with, and she could expect to receive them anytime. It made her feel small, insignificant. Just another woman. Was she crazy? She had trusted him with her deepest, most private self. It was stupid, a colossal mistake. But thinking she was in love with him was even worse. It was like deliberately running into a chopper and hoping to survive.

Trying to calm herself, she drank a glass of ice-cold water. Making love to Josh had been an unfortunate accident. A man-woman thing she'd been incapable of stopping. It wasn't going to happen again. And one way to make sure of that was to act as if nothing had happened between them. Withdraw. Never think of love. She scratched togetherness and cooking dinner and decided to make an excuse about work she had to do. He really looked out of place in her cheaply furnished apartment, and she wasn't about to redecorate. No, she would send him packing to his own ritzy quarters.

He came in carrying a huge shopping bag that squirmed and crinkled, and a white paper sack.

"I got takeout from Meet Me at the Mango." he said, and smiled an infectious smile.

He was setting the bags on her kitchen counter, telling her how hungry he was, so sending him away now would be awkward. As she set the table and unpacked the food, her little dining alcove filled with the delicious smell of spinach and cheese quiche and curried beef in green mango sauce with long-grain rice. He had also picked up a bottle of wine. He found the glasses by himself and poured. Bumpers lay down in a corner, watching them with affectionate eyes.

"Here's to a great day." He clinked his glass on hers.

Remembering was enough to steam her thoughts. "Did you like Meet Me at the Mango?" she asked.

"It's a really neat place," he replied. "The parrots in the cages started squawking when I took Bumpers in.

The maître d' got excited too, waving his hands—like this." Josh imitated the man. "It was wild. Bumpers threw in his little requests. Loudly."

She burst out laughing. He was funny and not as conservative as she had once imagined, or as George had led her to believe. Who else but Josh would take a dog into a restaurant?

"Then how did you manage to get the food?"

"I waited outside. No way was I going to leave Bumpers tied to a tree. The waiter brought the food out and got a handsome tip."

"Nice people," she said. "They go the extra mile. That's why they're doing so well."

They went on to eat their dinners, cutting each other generous portions from the quiches and raving over the curried mango, which Josh had never tried before but loved. The meat had a wonderful tang to it. The rice was delicately fragrant. They ate heartily. At last Josh looked up.

"You look beautiful," he said. "We're going to have to make sure you eat more curries from now on. Spices put a beautiful glow on your skin."

Her face tingled with new anticipation. His words pounded at her heart like ocean waves beating against a shoreline. And panic gripped her. She had to take control of her future, act fast to avoid sinking into the same pit she'd been in once before.

"It's the wine putting a glow on my face, and making me very tired." She yawned hugely. "I'm ready to call it a night. Bumpers and I thank you for dinner and we'll see you another time."

"Are you asking me to leave?"

"Yes."

"Are you sure?"

"Yes. It's been a long day. I have work to do. And I want to call my parents about a family matter. In fact, I have to call Aunt June, too."

He left her with a kiss and more misgivings than she would have thought possible. She had sworn off love and had a real goal—their family dream. She was dying to know if the investors had come through.

She called her parents, and her dad sounded more upbeat than she had heard him in a long time.

"I put a presentation together for the three investors I told you about. Two of them got scared off by inventory—they couldn't understand how we could compete with the chains. But one guy said he'd speak to his wife and get back to me."

Darcy cheered and hollered till her father said, "Hey, you're bursting my eardrums. June is here. You want to talk to her?"

Before Darcy could respond, her dad started wheezing and coughing into the phone. She held the phone away from her ear and worried, having learned a long time ago not to ask him if he was okay. That, her mother had pointed out, only reminded him that he wasn't.

Aunt June got on the phone. "We're going to bring Uncle Albert here for the day tomorrow, give him a break from the nursing home, since I'm over my cold and not contagious anymore. Your mother wants to know if you can join us. She's going to cook your favorite chicken and dumplings."

"I'll be there," Darcy replied, thinking she could bring Bumpers. "And I want to see those pictures of the store again. We have remodeling to do."

"We'll have to hire an architect," June responded. "Maybe we'll find a really handsome fun guy, and who knows . . ."

Darcy signed off in a rush, hung up the phone and groaned. She couldn't handle matchmaking or romance, but at least she'd taken control of her weak side and actually made Josh leave.

9

WELL, SHE'D SENT HIM packing. And he'd thought he'd won her over. Josh entered his apartment, feeling hurt and abandoned. After they'd made love, her eyes had been like a sunlit sky—she had glowed—and it had pleased him no end. The fact that she had withdrawn meant only one thing: Darcy was still in love with George. He swore aloud.

He had half a mind to call her up and ask her if that was true, but if she said yes, he'd be up a tree. Violent thoughts filled him concerning George. He considered driving over and pounding on her door till she let him into her apartment and her heart. She wanted to reset the clock, get back together with George. He didn't understand women. He wished she'd put the past behind her. George, from what he'd heard, wasn't about to divorce Rhonda and go begging Darcy for her hand. It was his parents who'd expected him to marry a nice girl like Darcy, and George had gotten in too deep, weakling that he was.

Of course, Josh couldn't point all that out to Darcy—it would only make her feel worse. But how, then, was he going to get her to stop loving George? No point in trying. All he could do was give her time to appreciate and love the better man for her, namely himself, and if that didn't work, he would have to accept it and move on.

He dialed the investigator, even though it was Saturday night, and much to his surprise, he answered.

"Still haven't turned up anything concrete on Billy Melrose, other than all those calls to Florida. It seems he talks in code. I've tried to break the code, but so far, no luck. He's very slick with his computer, too. Has so many handles we're trying to separate the serious ones from the diversions. And he's looking into buying a big boat."

"Has he applied for a loan?"

"No. He told the marina people in Chesapeake Bay he plans to pay cash. And the funny thing is, he didn't even ask the price."

"You may have to go to Florida. You don't have a clue as to where he's getting the cash?"

"No. He doesn't play the market, has no investments to speak of, other than his house in MacLean. That's worth $500,000 and it's all paid for. What I don't understand, Mr. Cartwright, is what he's doing riding the bus when he owns a Jaguar and a Mercedes?"

"That's why I hired you. Billy lives across the bridge in Virginia, and he was a regular on the D9, in D.C. I told you all this. I want you to get moving on it."

"Yes, sir. I'll go to Tampa next week. But, you know a lot of people drive into D.C. and then take the bus downtown to save on parking costs. You should be prepared to accept the fact there may be nothing illegal about Billy Melrose. Some guys just *act* shifty."

Josh got off the phone in a worse mood. The only positive so far was that Ginger's inheritance remained locked up till she married. And if Josh had his way, that marriage would not take place. He had to protect his sister. If he managed to get the goods on Billy, he could prove his suspicions to Ginger, and that would end it and the marriage plans. Then he'd have to find other reasons to convince Darcy to spend time with him.

Swearing, Josh picked up all the flyers and advertisements from his mail and tossed them into the wastebasket. Then he turned on the TV with the remote control and flipped through the channels, rejecting show after show. He decided to do a little work.

Work had always helped overcome his loneliness. He carried his briefcase to the desk, wrote a few memos and studied an associate's notes on the Vandenberg divorce. Mrs. Vandenberg was suing Josh's client, a distinguished economist, for divorce, and she wanted custody of their dog. Josh immediately thought of Darcy and Bumpers.

He'd left the dog with her, but he certainly wanted visitation rights, just as his client did. At one time Josh had suggested to Mr. Vandenberg that he get himself another dog, and the man had been incensed. In hindsight Josh knew he'd been downright insensitive and made a mental note to deal more sympathetically with clients and their pets next time.

It was too late to call the manager of his farm in Virginia, and he wished he could just take the time off himself and go fix the gutter spout and replace the shingles on the roof. But he knew he'd make a mess of it all, and that irritated him, too.

In bed he set the alarm clock and picked up an investment magazine to read, but Darcy appeared on every page. He could swear she cared deeply for him. She had responded with such wonderfully natural un- inhibited pleasure. Then she'd withdrawn. His stepfa- thers had warned him about female behavior, and his own observations and experiences had verified it. Women wanted you in the worst possible way and gave you their love, themselves, children, laughter and joy. Then it all ended in divorce.

Turning off the bedside lamp, he cursed George. Af- ter years of fantasizing about the slim beautiful enig- matic Darcy, he had managed to get close to her, get inside her. Hot and wet and welcoming. He cursed again. He should be with her now, holding her, loving her, but he had been sent away. Damn these women. He was going to make sure she understood he called the shots, not the other way around. And once was not enough.

And Josh stayed away on Sunday, hurt and angry at Darcy for pushing him out the door. He had other pressing matters adding to his headache. He wanted to pin Billy down, get him to answer some questions. And if he couldn't do that, he would ask Ginger about Bil- ly's Florida connections. Josh doubted she knew any- thing, but it was worth a try. He caught Ginger at home.

"I can see you for lunch, Josh, but I don't know about Billy. He had to go see one of his children yesterday. I'll leave a message on his machine to join us, maybe even later, for the Bullets game."

After he hung up, Josh swore. Billy led a whole sep- arate life from Ginger, and he bet Billy used his chil- dren as an excuse. Well, he would devote today to getting this problem with Billy sorted out.

ON MONDAY MORNING Bumpers woke her up, pressing his hairy face on hers, asking for his breakfast. When she simply rolled over, he started to bark. She bounded out of bed to feed him. "Yesterday you didn't have any fun without your friend, Josh, did you?" She set his bowl down. "Poor Bumpers, having to put up with Mitzi and Rambo. You hate cats."

As she ate toast, waiting for the coffee to perk, Darcy thought of what a nice family day they'd had yesterday. Her dad had suffered only one asthma attack, and she knew part of it was that the investors he'd talked about on the phone were definitely serious. And she'd loved talking about Phoenix, with its clear blue skies and crisp tan sand. She couldn't abandon Dreams, Inc., in Washington, D.C., but she hoped, over time, she could start operating more out of Phoenix and eventually move there. There was nothing to hold her in D.C.

Showered and dressed in a navy blue cotton suit with a tan blouse, she slipped on her high heels and grabbed her big canvas purse. "Bumpers, I hope I can fit you in here." He barked wildly. The doorbell rang and he jumped away, making menacing little runs toward the door.

She grabbed his collar to lead him into the bedroom, but he broke away from her, running circles around the living room. Afraid that the caller was her super, she tried to pick the dog up, hissing, "Sit. Sit," but he darted away.

"Okay, game's up," she said, and opened the door.

Josh slipped past her into the apartment, motioning her to lock the door. Bumpers bounded up to him and whimpered.

"Sorry, I shouldn't have rung the doorbell. Boy, he really has a loud bark," Josh said, planting a kiss on her cheek. "You look terrific."

It unsettled her that he didn't immediately hold her in his arms and kiss her like a lover. But she had sent him away. It really was best this way.

"I'm just leaving for work," she said. "Bumpers wouldn't get into this bag and went wild. I guess he likes the newspaper disguise better."

She had fantasized all night long about Josh. Once was not enough. There were so many positions she wanted to see him in, starting with his magnificent hard body stretched out below her. She wondered what would happen if she pulled off his beautiful red paisley silk tie and ripped off the expensive dark suit and stark white shirt. *Now*. She wanted to run her fingers through that springy mat of hair on his chest, kiss his thighs till he begged her to move her mouth, begged her to hurry and let him taste her. She remembered the burst of emotion that had hung between them and over them as they connected on every plain.

He'd been talking. "I'm sorry," she said. "I missed that."

"I came by to help with Bumpers. I have a nine o'clock staff meeting." He checked his watch pointedly.

She winced. "Go ahead. My car's parked down the block on the left. I'll follow."

"I'm in meetings all day, but I'll try to call you to see how things are going."

He set the dog in her car and left with a little wave. Darcy got in, steaming, and turned on the ignition. He had just treated her as though she'd begged for his help. Cold. Distant. A little peck on the cheek and a recital of his own important business schedule. Busy. Meetings. Those two words bugged her married friends the most, and when they talked about it, Darcy had fallen silent, pitying the poor housewives who didn't understand their husband's office life. Now she knew how patronized her friends felt.

By the time she got to the office, she had worked herself into a rotten mood and arrived frowning.

Everybody went crazy over Bumpers, petting him, lavishing praise, cuddling him, and he ate it all up, his big pleading eyes winning him instant fans. Darcy watched silently, glad Aunt June was bubbling with pity and love for the dog. It always helped to have your partner on your side.

Bumpers broke away from his admirers to bound up to Darcy, barking happily, bringing a big smile to her face. The dog definitely had a special way of chasing away her blues. He was cute and loyal and grateful.

"Oh, he loves you, Darcy!" one of her colleagues cried.

In her office Bumpers quickly made himself comfortable in a corner, and Darcy started getting down to business. She picked up listlessly where she'd left off. First she called a toy store and had a teddy bear sent to Antonio's grandson before calling Antonio to thank him for the dinner.

"How is your grandson doing?" she asked.

"Very well, thank you. And I am pleased you had such a good time. I am reserving all the carpets you requested." Then he hesitated oddly, and she wondered what was coming next.

"Mr. Cartwright will make a fine husband for you, Miss Darcy," Antonio said.

She chuckled and blushed. "I'm not looking for a husband, Antonio."

"God made women to have husbands, and Mr. Cartwright is a fine gentleman. Very honorable. A decent man."

Aunt June walked in as Darcy hung up. "You're as red as a beet. Was that a client yelling at you?" she asked.

"I'm not red as a beet. And that wasn't a client. What's up?" she asked, shuffling papers.

"Did Josh give you a date yet?" Aunt June inquired, apparently willing to overlook Darcy's abruptness.

Startled by the question, Darcy swiveled in her chair, mouth open, then she quickly leaned her elbows on the desk and said, "October sixth, and I meant to verify it with him when I saw him this morning."

"This morning?" Aunt June blinked, then broke into a big knowing smile and fingered her pearls.

"He stopped by before going to work to help sneak Bumpers out of my building. And that reminds me—I have to . . . to print out a poster," Darcy stammered. Why was everyone pressing Josh on her? He was a friend and a lover. She wasn't looking for commitment or marriage and knew she had opened herself up to an ocean of hurt, but she'd simply have to cope with it when they parted. And the thought of parting from

Josh depressed her no end. She rummaged through her desk drawers and came up empty-handed, just as she feared. She had no more candy bars.

Darcy typed, "FOUND—SMALL BLACK DOG," in seventy-two-point bold on her computer and then had to answer the phone. It was the Brass Barons informing her that the brass trays had been shipped and should be at her door that afternoon. The address the man verified was her own, not Dreams, Inc.

"How did this happen?" she asked.

"Your assistant said she was going to tell you," he replied. "Seems your office storeroom is getting pretty full."

She schooled her irritation. It wasn't that big a deal. The box could go in a corner of her living room. She heard the office doorbell ring.

"Florist," a cheerful voice sang out and her heart beat faster. Through the tumult, she heard her assistant gasp and a babble rise from her colleagues outside her office.

She ran out. "What is it?"

"The guy I met the other day sent me these roses. Aren't they beautiful?" Amy was so touched, tears were running down her face. Her last boyfriend used to hit her.

Darcy drew away, sneezing, remembering her sickly wilted wedding bouquet. She'd been expecting flowers from Josh. Maybe he just hadn't found time to send in his order yet.

The rest of the morning spun by as she worked on the details for Ginger's wedding. She called some of the biggest Italian and Greek restaurants and asked them for their catering lists and prices, having figured the smaller restaurants would have a tough time catering for five hundred people in Virginia and also running their daily business. The Dreams, Inc., cook, Rosa, had appeared extremely hesitant about her ability to cook Italian and Greek dishes in such great quantity, and with good reason. It was too big a project. She typed up her notes and shushed Bumpers for barking every time she turned on the printer.

At lunchtime, she called the Humane Society again and found no one had reported Bumpers missing. She took him for a walk and bought herself a salad. As she was heading back into her office, Aunt June caught her at the door.

"We have plenty of egg rolls in the kitchen left over from the Larrimer birthday. Take some home. And, oh, your mother called while you were out. She wants to bring over your favorite apple pie tonight."

"Mother got a new hairstyle?" Darcy laughed; her mother always baked when she got a new hairdo.

June laughed, too. "They're going to drop one off for me, too. Her hair was getting too long."

Leaving Bumpers with her aunt, Darcy drove to the spot where they'd found him and tacked the posters on a couple of nearby tree trunks. She dropped some off at the neighborhood stores, urging the owners to post them on their bulletin boards or cash registers.

Then she ran back to the office, expecting a message or flowers from Josh that would bear out her suspicions. There was nothing. A little puzzled, she threw herself back into work, but she might as well have printed up a poster—WANTED, JOSH, NOW—and nailed it to her brain. She tried to reason that he filled her mind because she was working on Ginger's wedding plans. She told herself that her warm and fuzzy feelings for him and the need to hear his voice had nothing to do with falling in love with him. She didn't love anybody or anything except her family and her work.

Nevertheless, picturing him sitting in his office sent her heart pounding. Was he distracted by that spot on his carpet where they'd made love? Was he thinking of her?

She lingered after work, jumping each time the phone rang or someone buzzed the front door. Finally, as she was leaving with Bumpers, Aunt June stopped her at the door.

"I have a bag here you can carry him in," she told Darcy.

It was a gym bag—long and low with a stiff bottom and sides. Bumpers fit in easily.

Much more confident now, she went on home. Her apartment building was quiet. A few lights were burning bright, but the hallway was empty. She rushed him into her apartment, and Bumpers went immediately to his water bowl and lapped thirstily.

She set a roast of beef, her dad's favorite, to defrost in the microwave, then quickly went to change and settle in for the evening. She wanted to surprise her parents with dinner and wished she'd stopped on her way home to pick up fresh rolls.

She thought again about Josh and sighed. He didn't fit into her plans. Buying back the Phoenix store would keep her too busy with her family. Her father's contacts, the investors, sounded extremely promising. With the ski wedding, the circus wedding and the Cartwright account, things were beginning to look up at Dreams, Inc., and she hoped she could offer some money for remodeling the hardware store.

Busy preparing the roast, sprinkling it with rosemary and pepper, she heard Bumpers growl even before the doorbell rang. She locked him up in her bedroom before going to the door, apprehensive about seeing the superintendent.

Josh stood there, in khaki shorts and an expensive-looking gold-and-white striped shirt.

"Hi." He smiled, lighting up the doorway and her heart. His brown eyes deepened to chocolate as his gaze swept over her.

"This was in the entryway." He pushed in a large wooden crate.

"They're Ginger's brass trays," she said.

He set the crate carefully at one end of the room, off the peach-patterned area rug. She let Bumpers out of the bedroom and he bounded into Josh's arms, licking his face, making him laugh. Josh's boyish enthusiasm made her smile. She left them frolicking and went to the drawer in the kitchen to get the pliers.

"Don't I get a kiss on the cheek? A little peck to say hello?" he teased when she returned.

Heart fluttering, she complied, limiting herself to a whiff of his musky after-shave and a taste of his freshly scrubbed skin. Firm. Smooth. Resilient. She didn't want to take the chance of running her fingers through his hair, because she knew she wouldn't stop till she'd contacted all his parts.

"You'll have to do better than that," he said, grabbing her and dipping her. Then he gave her a sexy probing kiss that filled her with passion and tasted so minty she thought wistfully of the carpet shop and all the things they could do together on those colorful patterns. If only she had gone ahead and followed her physical urges, she wouldn't still be fantasizing about making long hot love to Josh on the oriental rugs. Their Garden of Eden. Oh, what she would give to get locked up again—

"Darcy, Darcy, what am I going to do with you?" he said.

Her smile faded at his frown and drew her from her reverie.

"I'm upset about this," he said, dropping one of her posters on the table. "On my way home I saw your posters. With your name and number on them. Every damn pervert in town can now reach you, even show up on your doorstep. Didn't you think about that? Didn't it occur to you that you're putting yourself in jeopardy?"

"Wait a minute," she said. "No one's going to show up here, and if they do, I'll handle it."

He shook his head. "You look cute and a little ferocious. But you should be more careful."

Josh opened the crate with pliers, then pulled at the tape on the big plastic sheet that was wrapped around the contents. It made a swooshing sound, as some of the packing spilled out.

She grabbed newspapers from a table in the kitchen, ran back out and spread them around the box. Josh handed her the order form.

She read it aloud. "'Partial shipment. Brass table trays, wooden stands shipped separately.'" Then she said, "These trays should look authentic. I'm figuring six people could be seated around them on pillows." Remembering her own tumble into his arms from the pillow in Antonio's shop, she averted her face.

"So this is just the first shipment?"

"Right. I wanted to make sure Ginger liked them. Sometimes the workmanship is poor. Or the design might be awful. Or, the brass is so thin the trays are flimsy."

Reaching into the box, he scooped out an armload of plastic pellets and dropped them onto the newspaper. After taking more out, he groped in the box.

"They must have packed the trays deep so as not to scratch them," he said, pulling out another armload of the white pellets.

She stood over him, fighting back an impulse to tangle her fingers in his hair, tumble those dark waves, as he unpacked.

Inside the box, brass gleamed from small compartments. When Darcy leaned down to look, a groan escaped her.

"Trays, right," she said, picking one up.

He picked up another. They looked at each other. "These are coasters," Darcy said. "These aren't trays."

"Definitely not trays. Can you picture six people sitting around one of these?" He held one up.

She burst out laughing. "Not even dolls."

Josh picked up another brass coaster and started pretending they were castanets, banging them together.

His playfulness was infectious. Grabbing a small cylindrical vase off her table, she held it up like a microphone and burst into song. Her voice made a startled Bumpers run in circles.

Josh's eyes widened in surprise, then he leaned forward to harmonize into the vase/microphone. She was laughing too hard to continue singing and collapsed on the couch.

He sat down beside her and said, "You have a pretty voice. Antonio said you were a singing child. Have you ever considered doing it professionally?"

"And you play the castanets really well," she joked. "Have *you* thought about going on the stage?"

"We can form a band. Call ourselves Short Stops."

"Why Short Stops?"

"Because we're both wearing shorts," he said, rubbing his hand over her thigh.

The contact, his skin on hers, was electrifying and impulsively she said, "Okay, Short Stop," and rubbed her hand on his thigh, feeling his rougher skin and hard muscle below it. His thigh quivered and he gulped.

"This calls for a celebration. The Short Stops should go to dinner," he said, gazing deep into her soul, ruffling up her emotions.

"Sorry, I can't," she said.

"Then we'll have to celebrate in a different way." He pulled her to him and planted a flurry of kisses on her cheek. "We'll do dessert first."

She felt his warm lips and her own desire. He wrapped his arms around her and kissed her on the lips, nudging them apart and slipping his tongue in. She felt the moves it made all the way to her toes. Everything felt so right.

She pressed her lips to his, welcoming his deeper exploration, giving him her approval. He flattened his hand against her back and pressed her tighter to him, crushing her breasts against his hard chest. She moaned, overcome by desire, snuggling her face into his neck, smelling his masculine scent, nibbling on his earlobe, massaging a lock of his hair in her fingers.

The phone intruded loudly and she jumped back to reality.

"Let it ring," he said, clutching her hand. "Don't you have an answering machine?"

Before she could pick it up, the caller's voice filled the room. "Darcy baby, this is Martin. I miss you. It's been too long."

Josh slumped back, hair rumpled, breathing hard, looking accusingly at her.

Darcy grabbed the phone. Her dentist friend loved to exaggerate the description of their acquaintance. "Hi, Martin." Turning her back to Josh, she straightened her T-shirt, conscious of the damp heat from his mouth still lingering on her lips. "I'll call you tomorrow. Sure, lunch is fine."

When she hung up, Josh was sitting listlessly on the couch, a pillow in his lap, running a hand through his hair.

"So you're going out with Martin tomorrow?" he asked, obviously sulking.

"We're having lunch," she said casually.

Josh rose and started tossing the packing popcorn back into the crate and rattling the plastic sheet. "So how long have you two been going together?"

The tightness in his voice and shoulders surprised her. He sounded jealous. Josh jealous of Martin? Great bubbles of laughter filled her, and she bent to the floor, pretending to straighten the carpet, trying to get a hold of herself.

"Well, how long have the two of you been together?"

"Who? Martin and me? I met him a few months ago. He's a good friend."

"Friend? Somebody you confide in?"

She stood up slowly. So Josh didn't want her in a close relationship with another man, even if he was only a platonic friend. She felt so flattered she almost filled him in on her nonexistent relationship with Martin. But then again, the lady-killer didn't need to have his ego massaged back to its normal vast proportions.

Picking up the shipping slip, she dialed the company to leave a message on their voice mail.

Watching Josh repack the carton, she thought of how she liked, no, loved having him around. But he was getting too comfortable too fast here, all on his own terms. And it scared her, especially with this little streak of jealousy she'd just witnessed. The need to possess motivated rich and important men like Josh, so why had she let things go this far?

She wanted him to leave before her parents got here. They would jump to conclusions. "Josh, you should really get going. I'm expecting company."

He slammed the lid on the carton and straightened up. "You're expecting what's-his-name?"

"No. Martin and I are meeting for lunch tomorrow."

"A lunch date."

"I'll call you tomorrow evening."

"Darcy?"

He curved his mouth around her name in that special way of his, making her heart hammer.

"You really want me to leave?"

She nodded. He leaned forward to kiss her goodbye and landed a small peck on the cheek. She gulped and turned away. That brush of his lips tantalized her unbearably. It was insane to trust another man and jeopardize her carefully cultivated state of well-being, no matter how badly she wanted him to give her a lover's kiss.

She reached out and ruffled his hair. Smiling, he drew her into a tight embrace that brought a quick smile to her lips. This was more like it—a wild lover's proper goodbye, filled with affection and naughty intimacy.

He kissed her passionately again, and she tried desperately to hang on to her reserve. Well, yes, she had teased him and, well, yes, she was loving his kiss, but there was no point in opening herself up to dreams and promises that would be shattered. No point at all.

She pulled his head down and stroked his hair, rubbing her cheek ever so gently against his, making him groan aloud.

"I want to make love to you now," he murmured, "Say yes."

She flung her arms around him and he ran his hands through her hair, making her feel she had the softest most luxuriant hair any woman could hope to have. He cradled his cheek against it, and his breath puffed his anticipation across her neck, as he began to dispense with her clothing.

When he had cast aside the last piece of lace, he whispered, "You have a great body."

She offered it to him gladly. She lay down across the bed, head propped up on one arm, and patted the fresh sheet beneath her. "Hurry," she breathed.

He took his time undressing, watching her watch him, reveling in her eagerness. Then he knelt on the bed beside her, teasing her flesh with a hundred kisses, giving her access to his own pleasure points. She rubbed his chest, working her fingers through the mat of thick dark hair, bringing his male nipples to hard peaks.

He tumbled her on top of him, thigh to thigh, soft against hard, tracing a finger across her back, letting her press against his readiness. She groaned then, hungering for greater intimacy. Such a hard body. Such masculine warmth. Such tenderness and caring.

He entered her, filling all her senses with himself, taking them across sunny pastures and through treetops that blew and heaved to the roots.

Afterward he smoothed her hair back from her face and cradled her in his arms, enveloping her in a total sense of well-being. Catching herself drifting off to sleep, she scrambled up, alarmed.

"I forgot! My parents will be here any second!" She jumped off the bed and frantically gathered up her clothes.

Josh followed, reaching over to hook her bra, then dressing himself fast. She brushed her hair, applied a dab of lipstick, torn about having to ask him to leave.

"Josh," she began, trying to think of how she could do this without making herself sound crass. "Josh, I think—"

The whistling peal of the doorbell sliced across the room, snatching the words from her mouth and making Bumpers bark.

10

JOSH CURSED under his breath and grabbed the dog. She flung the door open to see her parents standing in the hallway.

"Come in," she said, smiling. "I love your hair, Mother. Short is better. Softer. It shows off your cheekbones. I wish I had your bone structure."

Her dad beamed. "Cora's been anxious to show you since eleven o'clock this morning," he said, setting the pie down on the end table.

"This family really *is* closeknit," Josh said, coming forward to greet Cora and Ralph. "Good to see you again."

When they saw him, their faces lit up. Josh pushed the packing crate out of the way. Then, smiling mischievously at Cora, he said, "I can smell cinnamon."

"Apple pie." Cora grinned. "My mother's recipe."

"My favorite," Josh said. "If you don't keep an eye on me, it might vanish."

"You must have some, Josh, I insist." Cora beamed. "Darcy, shall we order a pizza? You don't mind if we join you and Josh?"

"Josh was leaving. I was just about to put a roast in the oven," Darcy spluttered. "But if you're really hungry, pizza will be faster."

"Roast beef sounds better. Your mother's been on a pizza binge," her dad said, wheezing and pressing his fingers to his temples.

"I got tired of cooking," Cora said. "So I decided to bake."

"Makes a lot of sense," her father complained. "Wonderful pies and cakes and cookies. And we eat pizza for every meal."

"I guess I should be on my way," Josh said, settling firmly into his chair.

"Oh, no, stay," her parents chorused, avoiding Darcy's frantic eye signals.

"I'll get the roast started," Darcy said. Tight-lipped, she slipped into the kitchen, hoping her mother wouldn't come in and start pressuring her about Josh.

Her hope was in vain. Cora joined her less than a minute later. "Josh is talking football with your dad," she said. "It's a good thing they're both Redskin fans or we'd have to referee." Snapping beans, she edged close to her daughter and whispered, "See, I told you he's interested in you. Can't leave you alone, can he?"

"Oh, Mother. He's concerned about the dog, and we're discussing the brass trays for Ginger's wedding. And would you please not say too much about him and me, or it will make us sound like gold diggers."

"We're not gold diggers. Not even silver diggers, Darcy. You are far too conscious of that. We're proud people. We make our own way. You know all this. I shouldn't have to remind you."

"I guess I'm too conscious because of what George told me."

"Forget that ass. And don't hang on to anything George told you, because he told a lot of lies. And, oh, your dad wanted to surprise you, but since Josh is here, he won't mind my filling you in. This morning he met with the prospective investors, and all three are eager to buy into the property in Phoenix." She smiled. "They know your dad is an expert in the lumber business and want to invest on condition he expands the hardware store into a lumberyard. Of course, we don't mind that one bit."

Relief washed over Darcy. She hugged her mother and said, "I hated to admit it, but I had just about given up on it. The bank wouldn't give me a loan."

"You worry too much about all of us. You have to look out for yourself, you know."

"But I do, all the time. I take care of myself."

Her mother studied her fondly. "Darcy, as your mother, I have to tell you something important. Forget about whatever George told you. Josh is not like George. Josh wouldn't hurt a soul."

Darcy scowled. "George and Josh are cut from the same cloth, Mother." Cora meant well, but she just didn't understand the situation. It had grown even more complex from the second she'd let Josh seduce her, and now she glimpsed her future. Disappointment. Despair. The bitter triumph of being proved right again about her poor judgment when it came to men. She had read in a magazine once that women tended to make the same mistakes, go for the same type of man, over and over again. That was her, generally speaking. Except this time she was aware, and her goal was to end it.

Josh walked in. "Darcy, I can help, you know. Make a salad or something."

"Bless your heart," Cora said. "Here, you can finish snapping the beans." She shook a colander full of fresh green beans she had already snapped, then set it on the counter near Darcy. Pouring some peanuts from a jar into a bowl, she bustled out of the kitchen.

Josh moved closer to Darcy, put his arm around her, rubbed his cheek on hers. She could smell his aftershave and her lips seemed to quiver in anticipation of his kiss.

She bristled, pulling away. "My parents are in the other room, for heaven's sake." She picked up the colander, and emptied the beans into a pot.

"Sounds like the roast is in the oven," her father called out. "How about a cocktail?"

"Coming right up," Josh called back, then asked Darcy quietly, "Where's your bar?"

She chuckled, hung the dish towel on its hook and pointed to a small kitchen cupboard where she kept three bottles of liquor for guests. Josh sauntered out into the living room.

"Cocktail orders?" he asked her parents. She could hear the three of them talking together and laughing spontaneously, comfortably. It made her uptight.

Joining them, she pretended all was right with the world, but in the back of her mind, crazy images of Josh as a husband and a father, her parents' son-in-law, bobbed about like characters in a puppet show. And she caught herself giving the performance good reviews. Her stomach knotted.

"Considerate fellow," Darcy's dad said as Josh sauntered off to the kitchen to get the drinks, acting the gracious host.

Her parents were talking like little matchmakers again. Darcy groaned inwardly. She was telling them about the brass-tray fiasco when Josh reentered the room with the drinks.

"Your ice maker isn't functioning properly. I tried to fix it, but I'm afraid fixing things doesn't come naturally to me," Josh said.

"It's okay." Darcy smiled. "The building super also tried. He said a part is missing and he's ordered it." It surprised her that Josh would admit he couldn't fix things—till she remembered his privileged upbringing.

"You should see me try to fix my lawn mower," her father said. "Half the time I end up kicking it and hurting my foot."

Darcy went into the kitchen to get the egg rolls she'd zapped in the microwave, thinking how frustrating it must be for a competent take-charge man not to be able to fix things. When she came back, her parents were going on about their wonderful Greek meal at the Olive Basket. And Josh was gazing at her, deliciously spanning the distance that separated them, filling her head with him and all the tastes he offered.

"I'll go fix the salad," she said, unable to cope with the way her heart was reminding her that her mother was right. She was stubborn. Josh had demonstrated his sense of responsibility; he'd handled the dog—handled her—with consistent tenderness and extreme care.

In the kitchen she opened the refrigerator, brought out a head of iceberg lettuce and chopped it into a large glass bowl. While fancy lettuce, garnishes and exotic vegetables were all part of her day at Dreams, Inc., her home salads tended to be quick and plain. Today she wished she had some star fruit or papaya. She settled for peeling and slicing cucumbers and radishes.

She added the potatoes, carrots, tiny whole pearl onions and green beans to the roast and listened to the three of them talking in the living room. Their conversation was sprinkled with her dad's cough.

It had turned into a strange day full of little emotional surprises. Not to mention the source of said surprises. Josh lounged out there with her parents as though it was family evening time, as if they'd all done this for years. For a man who had grown up wealthy, Josh didn't act pretentious. Suddenly she was pleased he'd stayed for dinner.

"BOY, YOU'RE WORKING hard," Josh said when she returned to the living room. "Your parents were telling me what a naughty child you were, and I informed them that nothing has changed." He gazed boldly at her and communicated secrets—how she'd touched him, where she'd kissed him.

The oven timer pinged and she led them to the table. The meal she brought out was arranged beautifully, with a colorful ring of vegetables around the browned roast, which exuded a delicious aroma.

"This roast is done exactly the way I like it," Josh raved. "Just enough garlic and black pepper to give it pizzazz. Can I get some advice about meat loaf?"

"My grandma's recipe for meat loaf's wonderful," Darcy said, reaching for her water glass. "Dad's mother was a great cook. In fact, I use some of her recipes in our catering business. Her meat loaf, sliced, cubed and served on toast points, is a popular hors d'oeuvre."

"This may surprise you—" Josh chuckled "—but I'm on the board of a charity organization called the Community Kitchen. This year we decided to run a contest for disabled women over seventy. It's a way to boost their spirits. They send in their meat-loaf recipes, and our volunteers draw six winners every month."

"What a great idea!" her mother gushed. "What do the winners get?"

"Flowers from me," he said.

Darcy dropped her fork. That was his flower list? Meat-loaf-award winners?

"The idea was well received in the community," he said. "In fact, next year some other volunteer will send flowers."

She laughed so hard she rocked back in her chair, relief pouring through her. She'd been wrong about him.

"Let's have pie," her mother said, shooting Darcy a dirty look. After she'd served neatly cut slices, everyone ate quietly until Josh complimented her mother.

Darcy pulled herself together. "I'm sorry, Josh. You wanted some advice?"

He said nothing, ate the last crumb of pie and accepted a second helping. His shoulders finally relaxed.

"I was thinking of publishing a Community Kitchen cookbook eventually. Some volunteers could put it together to give these disabled women a boost but, from your reaction, Darcy, I guess we'll have to settle for a joke book," Josh said.

Darcy was slowly emerging from shock. She'd jumped to conclusions, imagining him sending flowers to women he went to bed with. And she'd caused herself endless pain. Well, it was all because of George and his stories about Josh. Which was one more reason to believe her mother was right in telling her to forget anything George had said.

"I'm volunteering to put the book together," she said. "It's a great idea and the women will like—"

"Okay," he interrupted her listlessly. "That's good to know." Deliberately, he turned to her father and started discussing automobiles—foreign versus American.

Darcy cleared the table, painfully aware that she'd offended him, yet unable to think of any way to redeem herself, short of fessing up about her convoluted flower theory. Hardly something she could discuss in front of her parents. She would have to make sure he stayed after they left. She'd tell him everything then and set it right. Between kisses.

But he walked out with her parents, tossing her a formal little thanks for dinner and goodbye. "I want to see your dad's new Pontiac," he said.

She didn't mind it, surprisingly. Josh *did* want to see the car, and his diplomatic way of handling her parents pleased her. He would came back after they left because she had made such a big deal out of down-playing their relationship in front of her parents.

An hour crawled by and he didn't return. She walked out and looked up and down the street, disappoint-ment coursing through her veins.

His Jeep was gone.

11

THE NEXT MORNING, dressed in her khaki suit and gold blouse, Darcy put Bumpers into the bag, ready to go to work. Just as she picked up her purse, the phone began ringing off the hook. Three people called, one after the other, to claim Bumpers. Asking them to stop by that evening, she rushed out carrying the bulging bag containing the dog, whose barking was muffled by the canvas.

Thankful not to see the super, she got behind the wheel of her car, unzipped Bumpers's bag and bent down to fasten her seat belt. A loud rapping on the window made her jump. Pushing the lock button, Darcy turned to see a face pushed against her window.

"You scared the hell out of me, Mr. Simmons. What are you doing?" she yelled, lowering the window a crack. Bumpers started growling and barking, and she almost groaned aloud, trying to invent another story.

"Your dog tape turned into a dog," Mr. Simmons said with a sneer. "Mrs. Parrish went for a walk and saw these posters." He held up a crumpled poster. "Now I'm seeing for myself."

"Isn't he a cute dog?" Darcy turned on the charm, but the super continued to glare at her. "Mr. Simmons, Bumpers won't be with me much longer. Three people are coming tonight to claim him. So I'll take him to work with me now, and you won't have anything to worry about."

"This is your last warning, Miss Blair."

"I'm going to be late for work. Goodbye, Mr. Simmons."

Bumpers had his foot caught in the bag and yelped piteously. She helped him out and drove on. Josh was right. She never should have put her name on that poster.

When she walked through the door to her office, a small voice said, "Hi," and Ginger waved at her from a chair; she'd been reading a magazine.

"Hope you don't mind my waiting for you in your office, Darcy." Ginger smiled shyly. "I work at a day-care center, but I asked my supervisor for the morning off."

"No problem. Good to see you. Coffee?"

Darcy went to the outer office and brought back two steaming cups and a couple of croissants.

"Josh wants Billy to sign these papers," Ginger said, her voice faltering.

"Many families request that. When two people are in love, like you and Billy are, it won't matter in the end."

"It's just that it makes Billy feel like he's not trusted." Ginger's lip quivered.

Troubled, caught between her boyfriend and her brother, Ginger was looking to Darcy for advice. Darcy was touched by that and that she'd taken time off from her job to do it. She was also impressed that Ginger wasn't idly waiting for her trust fund to kick in.

"Things work out. Maybe Josh can have lunch with Billy," Darcy said. "Have a man-to-man talk."

"Billy feels so bad he avoids Josh," Ginger blurted.

"Then you should have a talk with Josh. Tell him how Billy feels and how you feel. You can do that. And I know your brother loves you very much. He's trying so hard to do the right thing because he's older and feels responsible. He's a good guy. You should discuss how you feel with him."

Ginger's face clouded. "Well, I saw Josh yesterday, and he's worried about what Billy is doing in Florida. I told him Billy just goes there to see his father. But Josh said his father lives in Maryland. Frankly I'm getting confused. The only thing accurate so far is that Billy spends a lot of time at his computer. Josh doesn't understand it's Billy's hobby."

Darcy laughed. "So Billy is a hacker? He just needs to sit down with Josh and talk. Everything will work out. You can reassure him that your brother just needs to get to know him. And ask Billy what he does in Florida."

"I didn't see him this weekend." Ginger's mouth drooped. "I'll ask him when I do." She paused. "Darcy, you're so nice. I wish I had a sister like you. I wish you and Josh . . ." Her face lit up and she let the sentence dangle.

Darcy blushed. Everybody—her parents, Aunt June, Antonio and now Josh's sister—was matchmaking. Darcy hurriedly went on to talk about the invitations, leafing through catalogs full of samples, suggesting an artist she knew to design a fun yet elegant invitation. Ginger agreed enthusiastically and said she would call to set up a time to discuss her wedding dress with the seamstress.

"I'm glad Josh didn't insist on a rodeo wedding for me." Ginger sighed. "I can't ride a horse as well as he can, and I'm not sure Billy can ride at all. But a rodeo wedding is Josh's dream wedding."

Darcy changed the subject. After Ginger left, she continued working out the details of the wedding. An hour later she went into the kitchen to help with a bar mitzvah feast. Finally she took a break and went out for a walk with Bumpers.

It was a beautiful sunny day filled with the saxophonist's music and the flurry of lunchtime shoppers. She smiled as she passed Fred's Flowers. She had been ridiculous about Josh's list, torturing herself. The idea he would send flowers to only women he slept with had bugged her. In no way was jealousy involved. She couldn't be jealous of somebody she had no claim on, no expectations of, and she wanted to keep it that way, no matter how her opinion about Josh had softened.

As she walked by an outdoor café, she heard a familiar voice call out her name. With the sun shining so fiercely in her eyes, she couldn't quite see who was waving to her. She shielded her eyes and he came into view. She caught herself beginning to smile and reset her face. Those unmistakably mischievous eyes had always made her smile.

She reached his table and said, "George," in a thin voice.

"Yes. George Templeton. Remember me?"

Remember him? She clutched Bumpers's leash so tightly, her fingernails dug into her palm. Not once in two years had she run into George. Eventually she had quit anticipating a chance meeting, and that had alleviated her anxiety about what would happen and what she would say. She'd rehearsed so many speeches, silently and aloud, and it had drained her. The one thing she'd never wanted to do was cry in front of him. Right now there were no tears gathering.

"You look great. Do sit down," he said. "Would you like some coffee?"

He always had been quick with his offers of beverages and seduction, and she remembered loving that about him. "No, thank you," she said, thinking how, once upon a time, she'd actually thought he was a good lover. He'd been her first and he'd been a mistake.

"Didn't know you liked dogs," he said. "This one's well behaved." George pulled up the chair for her to sit down. "How long have you had him?"

"Oh, I've had Bumpers a long time," she lied, patting the dog and keeping one hand on his collar. The feel of his rough warm neck was somehow comforting.

"So. I finally get to meet you." The female voice came from behind her.

Darcy turned to see a fashionably dressed woman with long auburn hair looking curiously at her. She hadn't expected Rhonda to have such a plain but intelligent face. She'd imagined someone cheap and flashy, the type to ditch her husband and excite George into dumping her.

Rhonda slid into one of the empty chairs. A second glance registered the fact that she was older than George, probably by a good six or seven years. Fun-loving George had ended up with mama? The old hurt weighed on her.

"Hello," Darcy managed, but simply could not bring herself to shake Rhonda's hand. The woman had been George's partner in crime, hadn't she?

George sat grinning like a mindless fool. Suddenly it struck her that the things she'd found attractive about him before now turned her off. His boyishness now came across as bumbling immaturity. "How are you, George?" she asked.

"I'm fine," he stammered with a shifty glance at Rhonda. "I'm doing great." A strange expression crossed his face.

Remorse? Guilt? A sense of honor? She didn't think so. If he'd had any integrity at all, he would have told her personally that day. Face-to-face. Instead, he'd sent Josh to do his dirty work. He couldn't even take responsibility for his own actions. And he hadn't cared if she'd thrown herself off a bridge in a frenzy of hurt. At least she hadn't done that. And looking at his immature self now, was she sure glad she hadn't. He wasn't worth it.

"We read about you in *Bridal Ideas* magazine," George said. "Sounds like you're quite a celebrity."

"I'm a hardworking wedding planner," she said quickly, then wished her voice hadn't trembled. Why get defensive? About to add that life goes on, she thought better of it. Life hadn't just gone on in an uneventful way. She had built up an interesting career, found strength in herself and refound Josh, the thought of whom brought a smile to her face. Somehow she knew Josh and George no longer hung out together; they'd gone their separate ways.

George gave her an intense look, the kind that used to make her heart flip-flop. She just looked back, as she did at so many others all day long on the streets, in cafés, in stores—strangers who were part of the scenery but not part of her life.

"I heard you moved away, so the article was quite a surprise," George said.

"No. I stayed, George."

He looked away and rubbed his reddened face. She waited. After all, she had loved him once, thought him a wonderful human being. Surely he was going to attempt an apology? An explanation? A lie? He bent his head over his coffee.

It surprised Darcy that she felt nothing. She didn't burst into tears or crumple up with humiliation, nor did she deliver a tirade as she had always imagined she would. Why bother when she couldn't relate to George on any level? And she'd thought she loved this man? This wimp? This immature little ass?

There was nothing to be sorry or angry about anymore. Nothing to be gained by voicing her thoughts and stating the obvious. She took her leave graciously. "A belated congratulations to the two of you," she said, including George's wife in her smile.

Walking away, she thanked God she'd been spared. George had done her a favor, and never again would she look back and wallow in self-pity. She didn't have to waste one more minute on a man like him.

Back at the office, Darcy called to line up Portable Johns for Ginger's wedding and then tried the camel people again, but didn't get through. Her morning meeting had been moved up to the afternoon, and when the young couple arrived, hand in hand, she smiled at their youthful exuberance.

"We want a horseback wedding, with a fox-hunting theme," the woman said, and, then they filled her in on their dream wedding. Darcy was totally relaxed. Phoenix seemed so near, and it felt wonderful to have new wedding challenges. As usual she took copious notes, and when the meeting wrapped up, she was absolutely sure she could deliver, pleased that another account had come in. It wasn't quite as substantial as the Cartwright account, but the horseback pageantry would be exciting. She planned to get started on it tomorrow; it was to be a fall wedding.

After the couple left, Darcy called Josh, and his voice softened with pleasure when he heard her on the line.

"Three different people called about Bumpers," she told him. "They're coming over tonight. I thought you'd like to say goodbye to him."

"What? You gave total strangers your address?"

Okay, she'd done it again. But she'd been in a rush this morning, and the people hadn't sounded strange at all, merely concerned about a lost pet.

"You know, you could have met them at your office," he said. "What time are they coming?"

"No given time."

"Well, I'll come over after work. I don't care if you know karate or not. What if they're perverts?"

"Then they'll be so busy with each other, they won't bother me," she replied, trying to jolly him out of his anger.

"You're too trusting," he said in a serious tone.

After hanging up, she thought about her vow never to trust a man again. But maybe she was comparing a boy to a man. George, the boy, didn't belong in the same league as Josh. And the love she had felt for George didn't come close to what she felt for Josh.

At the end of the day, with a heavy heart, she drove Bumpers home to await his departure. The dog ate greedily and lapped thirstily at his water. After changing into black slacks, cream shirt and a casual black blazer, Darcy sorted through her mail—bills and ads and a postcard from a friend touring Europe. The doorbell rang and she sprang up, thinking Josh had arrived.

A small man with thick lips stood in her doorway. "I'm here to get my dog," he said.

Bumpers barked loudly and nipped at the man's ankles.

"Ouch. Stop it, you stupid mutt," the man said.

"I don't think this is your dog," she said as calmly as she could. The man's mean eyes and rancid smell repulsed her. "And he's not a stupid mutt."

"Hand him over and get down on the floor," the man snarled. "Now."

She held her ground, trembling. "Mr. Simmons," she called out, but her weak voice drowned in her throat. As she raised her leg to kick the man in a strategic spot, he pushed past her into the kitchen and started opening drawers. She hung on to an end table.

"The silver. Where's the silver?" he yelled.

"Only stainless steel," she spluttered. "I have no silver."

Having discerned that himself, he seized a carving knife.

She ran for the door, flinging it open, but the man grabbed her arm from behind. She screamed and Bumpers escalated his barking. Warning. Threatening.

"What the hell's going on?"

Josh! *Thank God.*

Next thing she knew, Josh had wrenched the knife out of the man's hand and Bumpers had clamped his teeth on the man's socks and was yanking with all his might.

"Call 911!" Josh yelled.

She snatched up the knife Josh had flung into the living room and made the call. Her voice got stronger as she reported her address. Josh had dragged the man in; he had one arm clamped across his throat.

"Check his pockets," Josh told her.

She found the task as repulsive as groping around in a public trash can. Hard pieces of bread. Cigarette butts. Matted old tissue. Things damp and slimy and reeking of rot. No gun or weapon. No wallet. Then she checked his pant cuffs, which were filled with dust.

"He told me to get on the floor," she said.

"That's what you're going to do, buddy. On your face." Josh pushed the man down, and Bumpers jumped on him and grabbed the back of his dirty gray shirt with his teeth. Josh planted himself out of reach and said, "One move and I'll shoot you."

Good strategy. She applauded Josh with her eyes. He didn't have a gun, but the man didn't know that.

Within minutes two policemen arrived, took statements and made an arrest. The man was a vagrant and he wasn't talking.

After they all left, Josh took Darcy in his arms and said, "Darcy, you have a facility for drawing criminals."

"Are you counting yourself among them?" she asked.

"Sure," he said, and laughed. After a moment he said, "We'd better pull ourselves together. The others who called will be showing up, and anyone else who managed to look up your address in the phone book. The city's crawling with robbers and worse...." At the look on her face, he changed his tack. "How was your lunch with Martin?" he asked.

"It was canceled. I was going to fix him up with Amy, but she wasn't interested."

Her running into George wasn't worth a mention. And here she sat, so friendly to George's best friend. How had all this happened? She had planned to tell George off, but she hadn't done that, either. It would have been like screaming at a dishrag. Pointless. She knew now that he had done her an enormous favor.

"Would you like to have a Coke?" Josh asked. "Don't get up. I know where things are." His face had lit up at the news that she'd cancelled her lunch with Martin, and he began to hum.

Sinking back into her chair, Darcy closed her eyes. It was so comfortable, Josh protecting her, taking care of her. His presence brought peace, along with the pandemonium. She smiled, taking the glass he handed her and rattling the ice cubes mischievously.

He laughed and rattled his ice back. The phone rang and he picked it up. After listening quietly, he said, "Thanks for calling. I'm glad it's worked out for you."

Josh sat down beside her. "Two down. One to go," he said, sipping his Coke. "These people were okay. Their dog showed up this morning, so they wanted to let you know they're not coming. Now, we wait for the third so-called owner. Incidentally I got up early and took down all your posters. Then I sent my assistant to the shops to retrieve them. He got about twenty of them."

"Sounds about right," she said in a low voice. "I wasn't thinking when I put my name and number on them. That was stupid."

"Live and learn," he said. "So, how about I order Chinese?" At her enthusiastic nod, he dialed the number and placed an order, then sat back and mused, "You know, growing up, I always fantasized about closeknit families gathered around the dinner table, sharing ideas, stories about how their day went. And I imagined they always ate big wholesome dinners with three vegetables and homemade pie to top it off. Ginger and I ate pizza in the kitchen."

She chuckled. "Most kids would love that."

Sadness dimmed his eyes. "Tell me about growing up. I know you went fishing with your dad. What else?"

"Oh, we had a lot of family picnics. On Mother's Day, Dad and I would cook all three meals, starting with cheese omelets and ending with a strawberry shortcake. And we watched old home movies. On Father's Day we'd go fishing early in the morning and have hot dogs and fried chicken for dinner. Sounds like a lot of food, doesn't it?"

He lowered his head. "Sounds like another world," he mumbled. "In our house there were no family traditions. Just constant change. Our stepfather would do his own thing on Father's day, with his own children. He'd accept our small gifts, and then Ginger and I would sit in the kitchen and eat leftovers. Slim pickings, because my mother thought cooking was a waste of time. On Mother's Day, she went out."

He'd lived a childhood of uncertainty about belonging in a family. It saddened her, made her want to comfort him, but instinct told her to keep her distance; pity would embarrass Josh. She was proud of how he had emerged from that neglected childhood as a compassionate human being.

There was a loud rapping, and Josh opened the front door. A gray-haired man in an expensive gray suit stood there looking tentative. "I've come about my dog. I'm so upset. Don't know how he got away, but I think the realtor had something to do with it. She's not a dog lover, and I'm certain she left the garage door open when she was showing a prospect around," he explained hurriedly. "Where is he?"

Josh shot Darcy a reassuring look and allowed the man inside. Bumpers ran straight to him and he bent down to pet the dog. "I'm afraid this isn't Sam," he said in a low tone. Bumpers barked with joy. "But he's a handsome devil. A friendly sort." He shook their hands and left.

Josh locked the door and rushed back to Darcy. Picking her up in his arms, he yelled, "Bumpers doesn't belong to him!" He roared with laughter.

Darcy joined him. "He belongs with us," she said.

Their dinner arrived and they sat down to a wonderful aroma of garlic and soy sauce and sautéed scallions. Josh spooned a sampling first on her plate, then on his own.

"I don't think anyone is looking for Bumpers," he said, taking a sip of water. "Waiting for him to be taken away has been entirely too tense. I haven't even kissed you yet."

He'd voiced her exact sentiments. Her heart hammered. "Later." She winked and picked up her chopsticks.

12

"FORTUNE COOKIES!" Josh placed a cookie by her plate. "You go first."

"No, you first," she said.

He snapped his cookie in two, pulled out the paper, read it and grinned. "Cool. This says, 'Your persuasive manner is at an all-time high.' What does yours say?"

She read silently and felt the heat rush to her face. She went to tuck the slip of paper under her plate, but he pulled it from her fingers and read it aloud. "'Think hard and move softly.'" He fell silent, ran fingers through his hair, then grinned. "Have you ever wondered if these fortune cookies are really on the mark?"

"They're just for fun," she said, rising to clear the table. *Think hard and move softly.* The word "hard" was doing a number on her, making her wish softly for his closeness. She wanted to do the bold thing and test for hardness, see if the cookie was on the mark, but that wasn't her style. No point in leading him on, or herself, for that matter. They were getting awfully cozy, and she wasn't complaining about that, but she had to wonder—without Ginger's wedding to plan and with Bumpers gone, where exactly would her relationship with Josh be? This affair would end soon, and the sooner the better.

He came into the kitchen, propped his finger under her chin and gazed into her eyes for a long moment, tumbling her composure. "Hmm, why aren't your arms around me? I thought I was at my all-time persuasive high."

"You're reaching too hard for that joke." There, "hard" had bounced up again. She whirled away, feeling the blood rush to her face. "Oops, I'm supposed to move softly," she said, tiptoeing to the door, knowing she was flirting and not minding it a bit. She suddenly wanted to live today, go with the flow. Tomorrow she would distance herself.

"Here, let me try this technique..." He took her hand, tucked it under his arm and began leading her to the bedroom, with the style and swagger of an English duke.

She enjoyed the fleeting image of taking off her clothes behind a silk screen, removing the hat from her head and shaking her hair loose. But this was here and now, and she wasn't wearing a hat. Neither was the man she wanted. "Interesting technique," she commented, and darted back into the living room.

He strode in, caught her, picked her up and hoisted her over his shoulder. "Is this persuasive enough for you?" He squeezed her bottom deliciously.

She wriggled and nibbled his earlobe, whispering, "No. I don't play trophy for a caveman. Put me down."

He did with the exaggerated groan of a primitive man. "Now let me try something else here..." He rubbed his chin villainously.

She watched with building excitement, waiting to see what he would do next. Her heart pounded. The glow in his brown eyes melted over her like chocolate.

"It's not *hard* to move softly," she said, fluttering her fingers like butterflies across the front of his trousers. "I can do this softly. Here, let me show you again." The fabric rose up against her barely moving fingers, and she fluttered them across, this time like birds across a tree trunk.

Relishing the way he groaned and tightened his grip on her, she leaned down and softly brushed her hands over his thighs, then down his calves, deliriously aware of how his legs quivered beneath her touch. At last she groaned, "You're persuading me. Carry me away."

He picked her up and tossed her over his shoulder as he'd done before, but this time she didn't protest. She was eager to have him and hold him and openly share the raw emotions that ran like currents between them all day long and turned into rivers at night.

He took her into the bedroom, breathing hard against her legs, then set her on the bed and joined her even faster than she'd hoped. She didn't remember how the clothes came off. She didn't remember where she flung her shoes. All she knew was his tongue, his fingers. He whispered sweet nothings in her ear, and her body reacted with wide-open love as she pressed her lips feverishly to his.

He took great pleasure from her fingers, groaning her name in a husky voice that reminded her of the creak of a sailboat tied to a dock. She paused her fingering, exploring, savoring, to absorb his voice, absorb him.

And he obliged.

Eagerly, passionately, he thrust himself in her, and she closed her eyes and clutched all he had to offer. Sated at last, they lay together, sharing a wordless satisfaction.

After a while she woke up, suddenly realizing she'd drifted off to sleep in Josh's arms. He felt her move and urged her toward him.

The phone and the doorbell intruded loudly, both at once. She picked up the phone first. After a moment she handed the receiver to him.

"Josh, it's Ginger. She sounds very upset."

Quickly throwing on her clothes, Darcy went to the door. Mr. Simmons stood there looking indignant. He cast a dirty look over her shoulder at Bumpers.

"Mrs. Parrish says this place has become a zoo. Says the cops were here. I was at the hardware store, so I missed all the noise. What's going on?"

She wanted to say that Mrs. Parrish should get a life, but she bit her tongue. "A vagrant burst in here and tried to steal the silver," she said.

After seeking a few more details, Mr. Simmons got to the point of his disgruntlement. "We want the dog gone by tomorrow morning."

"Tell Mrs. Parrish the dog hasn't been claimed yet, and I need time to make other arrangements."

"You ain't getting more time. When you get home from work tomorrow, you better not have it with you, or I'll have to take measures."

She hated threats, but there wasn't anything she could do. She was in the wrong, and arguing would only make matters worse. Shoulders slumping, she said, "Okay, Mr. Simmons."

Closing the door, she turned around to see Josh hanging up the phone. He looked wild-eyed, running both hands through his hair. "It's Ginger," he explained. "Billy's been arrested for fraud. I knew it. I just knew the guy was up to something. I've got to go."

"Let me go with you, Josh."

"I heard the super's ultimatum, too. You'd better stay with Bumpers or he'll bark his head off. This may be a long night." He put his hands on her shoulders and said, "I'm worried about you answering the door. Do *not* answer the door. You don't know who's going to come stumbling in out of the night." He was talking fast. "Don't try to take Bumpers out in the morning by yourself. I'll be here by six-thirty."

He kissed her briefly but tenderly and admonished her again not to answer the door.

After he'd rushed away, Darcy locked the door and sat down, shocked. So, Josh had had good reason for being suspicious of Billy. Poor Ginger. Betrayed by a man she trusted. Her heart went out to the young woman.

Forcing herself to deal with the business at hand, she called several acquaintances to see if she could place the dog with them, but there were no takers.

"Come on, Bumpers, time for bed," she said, picking up the snoozing dog. "Don't worry, I won't give you up, even if I have to check you into a hotel."

Sadly she remembered that hotels didn't allow pets, either, and they were expensive. But he could go into a kennel. She smiled, settling him on an old green comforter in the corner of her bedroom. He couldn't live in a kennel forever, but the short-term solution brought her immense comfort.

Now Josh filled her mind. Her lover. Her friend. Her harbor. He fit into every facet of her life, brightened it, and there was a canyon of emptiness when he wasn't around. She was attached. The steel wall around her heart had mysteriously crumbled, letting her love for him filter through.

Was it love? These intense feelings were making her vulnerable. She had to untangle herself, get herself free before craziness set in and her expectations rose.

But it didn't hurt to dream. It was so much easier to dream. With dreams she could cope.

"Josh, I love you," she whispered into her pillow, imagining their life together. Excitement. Laughter. Sharing. Raising a family, the kind of family he'd never had. Pointless speculation, she cautioned herself. And she worried about him, amidst Billy's mess and trying to console his sister.

WHEN SHE WOKE UP, he was there. It was barely six o'clock and still dark when she heard Bumpers bark. Then the doorbell rang. "Coming," she called, grabbing a robe and finger-combing her hair.

He came in smiling, but the circles under his eyes and his slumped shoulders told another story. He carried a paper sack of fresh croissants that smelled divinely. After one sharp little yelp, Bumpers jostled Josh lovingly.

"Tell me about it, Josh."

He leaned on the counter, distraught. "It's a mess. I had to do the most difficult thing in my life—disappointing Ginger. I refused to post bail for Billy. He's involved in a complicated fraud scheme. He's been bilking old people out of their savings, selling get-rich-quick schemes."

She placed a hand on his arm. "How's Ginger holding up?"

"Not too well. Good thing she had to go to work. The poor kid. She couldn't understand Billy's doing something so mean and cruel. The showdown came when I refused to pay his bail and Billy ordered her to pay. He wouldn't accept the fact that her trust fund is tied up, and would you believe he told Ginger he wouldn't marry her if she didn't come up with the bail right there and then?"

Sympathy for Ginger brought tears to Darcy's eyes. She turned away to make coffee.

"I was proud of Ginger," Josh went on. "After sobbing her heart out, she threw the ring in his face." He shook his head. "I'm sorry, Darcy. The wedding is off. You don't need to return the deposit."

"You think that's what's uppermost in my mind? Of course we'll return the deposit. You put down far more than you needed to."

"I didn't mean to make you mad, Darcy. I'm just sorting through things myself. This is one time when I wish I had been wrong. I hired an investigator who fell down on the job, then came running into the police station with some of the same information as the FBI got weeks ago. So I don't exactly feel hiring him was a smart move."

"Come here, Josh. Sit down." She led him to a chair at the dining table, hugged him for a long time, comforting him, then went back into the kitchen and returned with two steaming cups of coffee and croissants. "What can we do to help Ginger? Should I go see her? I can take Bumpers to a kennel on my way. I've decided to move someplace where they accept pets."

"You don't have to do all that. I talked to my farm manager in Flint Hill. I hated asking him, but he'll keep Bumpers there. You can visit him whenever you like."

Visit? So, he didn't want anything more than sex, after all, not that she had commitment in mind.

The doorbell peeled. "Mr. Simmons, no doubt." Darcy sighed and went to the door.

A young blond woman holding a baby, a little boy at her side, stood there. The little boy squealed, "Primer!" and Bumpers vaulted over Darcy's feet and barked so joyously, Darcy knew she'd lost the dog. The baby smiled and cooed.

The boy began running around the living room with Bumpers prancing beside him. "Watch this," the kid said. Then he got down on all fours, and Bumpers jumped over him. As boy and dog played, Darcy's heart sank.

"I'm Martha Jarvis, and I can't begin to thank you enough for taking in Primer. We were away in Hawaii, and when we returned day before yesterday, the house-sitter, who's an irresponsible young man, told us he was missing."

As Martha described the shock and anxiety her family suffered, Josh put his arm around Darcy, who fought back tears. Clearly the dog belonged to these people, but still determined to be sure, Josh called, "Bumpers, get over here! Bumpers!" The dog halted his play briefly, glanced at Josh as if to say, "I hate that name," then resumed playing leapfrog with the boy.

Darcy wiped away a tear. The dog's eyes were shining; there was no more pleading in them, and she was glad. His past was restored. But it saddened her that he was leaving, and it hurt that he had transferred his affections so quickly.

"He is lovable, isn't he?" Martha said. "And Posy is even friendlier than Primer. She'll be happy to have him back. She's been whining and refusing to eat."

Josh brightened. "Do they have any puppies?"

Martha laughed. "Even the mailman asked us that," she said. "But they've been fixed. You can visit him, though, if you want."

Darcy's last ray of hope fizzled. *Visit?* She could visit Bumpers. She could visit her friends' babies, her parents' cats, Aunt June's parrots. A feeling of emptiness engulfed her. She hugged Bumpers goodbye, and he licked her face in parting gratitude, but immediately rushed back to his real friend, the little boy.

After they were gone, Darcy picked up her purse and keys. "I have a meeting to go to, and I'm awfully late," she told Josh.

"Wait, you look really upset. We should be happy that Bumpers found his family. Your posters did pay off in the end—Martha had one sticking out of her purse. And Bumpers looked so glad to see his buddy...."

She nodded, thinking about the boy—and the baby, sorely reminded her of her mother's lectures about the ticking of her biological clock. "You should find yourself the right guy and settle down," she was forever saying.

After running into George yesterday, she knew for sure she'd found the right guy. But Josh hadn't mentioned love or a commitment. And maybe he never would. Surprised to find herself even thinking in those terms, she sipped her coffee. It was the way of men. Look what Billy had done. He'd proved to Ginger that all he loved was her money. And no matter what her heart said, why should Josh be any more sincere?

"I'd like to go see Ginger. Another friendly face might help."

Josh smiled. "She'd like that. But I think after work would be better. Would you drive out to my farm with us tonight?"

"I'd be happy to." Darcy returned his smile. "I know how Ginger feels, but it's a good thing she found out about Billy now."

The two of them went down to the parking lot. Before she climbed into her car, Darcy smiled again and said, "I'll see you after work."

DEEP IN THOUGHT about all that had happened, Josh didn't even realize where he was walking until he heard the saxophonist and smelled the snapdragons set up in front of Fred's Flowers. Darcy's genuine concern for his sister touched him. She was everything he'd imagined her to be and more—warm and genuine and caring. As he passed the small jewelry store in the next block, he dallied so long in front of the window that a salesclerk waved at him from within. Josh quickly moved on. What if she said she still loved George? He couldn't handle it.

He remembered the ring George had given her, and how he'd confided in Josh that poor dear Darcy didn't even know it wasn't a real diamond. It had been a large and square solitaire, and at that time Josh had thought the size impressed Darcy. Now he understood Darcy couldn't have cared if it had been made of clay. There was nothing calculating or shallow about her. Hers was a solid world of trust and honesty, family stability and good all-American traditions he hadn't even begun to explore yet.

He was ambling down cobblestoned P Street when he ran smack into George. He fought a sea of emotions. Darcy had turned away from him because of this man, and she continued to reject him. George was with the same red-haired woman he'd been with the night before he jilted Darcy. The woman he'd married. Josh grimaced. George had known better than to ask him to be his best man again. Good thing.

"Hey, Josh! Thought you'd disappeared off the face of the earth, man. Where have you been hiding?" George pumped his hand and laughed a little sheepishly. "Remember Rhonda? Guess you heard we're married now."

Josh smiled to see George squirming. The jerk. George had somehow known not to contact Josh after the day he'd left Darcy at the alter.

"The old gang says you don't come around anymore. Remember those wild parties we used to have? And speaking of that, I saw Darcy yesterday."

Panic seized Josh. Darcy hadn't said anything about meeting George, and he'd thought he had a handle on what she was up to. He wanted to grab George by the scruff of his neck and shake him. Instead, he plunged his hands into his pants pockets. "You saw her yesterday?" he asked, his voice controlled. "Did you have lunch?"

Rhonda shook her head. "Darcy must finally be over George. You know it's not very nice knowing somebody hates you, but yesterday I didn't sense any hostility from her. She just congratulated us, and I think she meant it."

Josh took a deep breath. He wouldn't bother explaining to Rhonda that Darcy was a lady—intelligent and beautiful. His heart filled with warm happiness knowing he was friends with such a woman. And if she'd congratulated George, she had to be over him, unless, of course, she was outwardly making the best of a bad situation and simply being polite. Suddenly he had to know something of tremendous importance.

In a calm voice, editing out the harsh words he really wanted to hurl at the couple, he asked George, "Did you think she was upset seeing you again?"

"Hell, no!" George shook his head. "She acted as though she didn't know me at all. I asked her to sit down, but she had a dog with her and said she had to go." George moved closer and continued, "I'd been telling Rhonda to expect a scene from sweet little Darcy Blair if we ever ran into her. But she surprised us. Said nothing. It was almost as if she didn't care."

Josh grinned. "She doesn't care," he said, then more loudly, "She doesn't care."

George shifted from one foot to the other. "Why don't you and Rhonda and I go to dinner tonight? Talk over old times."

Josh drew another deep breath before speaking. "Sorry, George. I'm not free for dinner." *Not now or any other time.* "I don't think we have anything in common. Now, if you'll excuse me."

Josh walked away rapidly. And about twenty yards down the street, he did a little jump. *Darcy doesn't love George.* He wasn't even important enough for her to mention.

He started walking back toward Darcy's apartment, where he'd parked his Jeep on the street. He thought how George hadn't grown up at all. Looking at his pale face and glazed eyes, listening to him and Rhonda, he'd felt sorry for George. The man had thrown away his life on drugs and parties and sunk family money into useless businesses.

Passing the saxophone player, Josh dropped a twenty-dollar bill into his hat, drawing an appreciative grin from the musician. He went into Fred's Florists. "I'll take five dozen red roses," he said. Three for Darcy and two for Ginger to cheer them up on the drive to Flint Hill. Carrying the armload of tight fresh roses, smelling their sweet fragrance, he began walking quickly.

He wanted to show Darcy his farm. He wanted to share his past, show her his room, tell her so many things. He broke into a jog.

13

DARCY PACKED a small overnight bag when she got home to an apartment quiet as a tomb. The lease on this place was up in two months, and she would move and get a dog like Bumpers. Despite Ginger's wedding being canceled, things were looking up at work. Today a request had come in for a library wedding, where each guest would receive a five-foot-high book cover of their favorite book, which they would stand behind in a big hall.

She laughed, rethinking that conversation. The young man who'd come in with the security deposit had said, "A famous author is marrying his secretary, so we don't want any details to get out, and they won't tell you yet which books the bride and groom wish to dress as. This will be a literary event."

The idea tickled Darcy's fancy. She loved her job. Between the weddings and the smaller events the others at Dreams, Inc., had lined up, she didn't have to worry. The whole year was filling up nicely. And she was willing to get to know Josh better. Finished packing, she brought her bag out and set it by the door. Missing Bumpers, she called Aunt June, who was at home with a cold, to tell her about the new wedding assignment.

Aunt June congratulated her. "I knew that magazine article would bring in business, and it's all thanks to you."

June didn't sound like herself, and Darcy asked, "Is something wrong?"

Unhappiness came flooding across the line as her aunt drew in a sobbing breath. "I got my divorce-settlement check today. He didn't even enclose a note, so I called him last night. I thought I would be able to reopen the lines of communication and invite him to dinner."

Darcy's heart sank. She had no kind memories of her self-important uncle.

"He said he's getting married again and didn't even ask how I was doing."

After consoling her aunt, Darcy added her ex-uncle to her list of rotten males. Betrayal and cruelty ran rampant among men and she wasn't about to give Josh a chance to get to that point. If it wasn't for Ginger, she would begin her disassociation now. Her heart crumpled. Okay, so it wouldn't be easy but she could do what she'd done before—throw herself into her work. Thank God, there was plenty of it.

Josh arrived with Ginger, and Darcy hugged the brokenhearted young woman as she wept.

It took an hour for Ginger to pull herself together, and Darcy talked softly to her the whole time.

"Listen to Darcy," Josh said. "Everybody can make a mistake. It's all part of growing up."

Darcy shot him a surprised look. "What mistake have you made?" she asked.

"Letting my loyalty get the best of me."

Darcy couldn't decipher his cryptic words and wondered if she should probe. Well, he had witnessed her humiliation. Turnabout was fair play. "Who were you loyal to?" she asked.

"George," he said. "The day I met you I wanted to take you out, but George told me to stay away. And I did the gentlemanly thing."

Darcy's mouth fell open. "George told me you advised him against marrying me. He also said you were a playboy. I assumed that all those flowers you sent were for your girlfriends. Uh, I mean, I thought you sent them flowers after you got to know them . . . well."

He laughed long and hard. "You didn't think . . ." He glanced at Ginger.

Darcy continued, "Well, George said—"

Josh swore, cutting her off. "After the bachelor party I drove him home and, uh, Rhonda, was waiting for him. She announced her husband had agreed to a divorce. I should have yanked him out of there. I should have made him live up to his responsibility."

She saw the anguish in his face, and her heart melted and filled with new emotions. Josh was loyal to a fault. He couldn't possibly have been responsible for George's actions.

"I'm glad you didn't, Josh. I saw him the other day and was so relieved I hadn't made the biggest mistake of my life."

"And here I thought you were in love with George all this time."

"Well, he did a number on me. I never could understand what I had done to deserve such treatment. And

I couldn't forgive myself for my poor judgment. How could I have loved and trusted a man like George?"

"You were young, and George kept his affair with Rhonda a big, big secret—even from his closest friends. I knew they'd gone out a couple of times but I had no idea he would do what he did."

Darcy heard Ginger his sister begin crying again, and she swung around. "Oh, I'm so sorry Ginger. We don't mean to talk about old times. Here." She grabbed a tissue for her. "We should be more sensitive."

Ginger wiped her eyes. "No. I'm crying tears of joy. You got over George and it gives me hope I can get over Billy. Now I'm hoping you and Josh will get together."

As Josh's eyes rested on her, Darcy's heart filled with happiness. She knew now he really cared about her. "Come here," he said, reaching a hand out in each direction.

He embraced the two women. "Shall we go?" he asked.

Disappointment filled Darcy as they walked out. She would have liked to have heard him say, "I love you."

They got in his Jeep, fragrant with the sweet smell of the roses stacked on the back seat. "For you and you," he said, handing each of them a bouquet.

Darcy held the roses in her arms and breathed deeply.

"Josh, Darcy," Ginger said, "I'm going to be brave. I have to pull myself together. So don't let me keep talking about Billy." Then she burst into tears.

Darcy and Josh exchanged startled looks. "Okay," Darcy said, "we won't talk about any jerks. We'll talk about something irrelevant, like llamas."

"Llamas?" Josh exclaimed. "What about llamas?"

"They're ugly. My grandfather was one of the first in this country to own a llama. He owned a hardware store in Phoenix, and during the depression a customer who couldn't pay gave him a llama. Then word got around, and the zoo came to collect two days later."

"You think they're too ugly to have around?" Josh asked.

"No. I think they're fun."

Josh smiled broadly and looked in the rearview mirror at his sister, who giggled, wiping her eyes. "Josh has always wanted to raise llamas, Darcy."

"Your grandfather's hardware store was in Phoenix?" Josh asked. "I didn't really know where your dad was raised."

"It just happens that he's going out there soon to buy the store back," she told them, and then related the wonderful news about the investors.

"You should have told me about this before. Do you need another investor by any chance?"

"No," she said. "But thanks for asking."

Josh reached over and placed his hand over hers. Other women he'd known would have expected him to bail out their families, advance them money, offer collateral, obtain expertise from his law firm free of charge. But Darcy hadn't breathed a word of what was troubling them as a family. "You're something else, Darcy—determined, hardworking, efficient, independent."

She groaned and waved a hand. "Oh, stop it!"

"Are you planning to move, too?" Josh asked.

"Eventually," she said.

Josh let go of her hand and placed his own back on the steering wheel, his face set in hard lines.

About ten miles farther, the Blue Ridge Mountains suddenly brightened the skyline. The apple orchards sprinkled across the foothills of the cobalt mountains added a rich texture of dark and light greens. Hardwood forests punctuated the landscape farther down the road. Darcy hadn't been out this way for at least three years, and she sighed, thinking she ought to do this more often.

Josh turned off on a dirt road that meandered upward, with stone fences leading the way to an elegant redbrick Victorian mansion with eight chimneys rising to the treetops. The driveway was lined with boxwood and led to an old-fashioned porch, with white gingerbread trim.

"Wow," she said, imagining the past grandeur of the home, the flurry of butlers and maids. Antiques and brocade. Chandeliers. And it made her heart sink. This was what surrounded Josh as a child? She knew the Cartwrights were wealthy, but *this* wealthy? This was far more opulent than anything George's parents owned. Nervousness rose within her as she compared this to her own simple background, but then she reminded herself that the wealth had not given Josh a happy childhood.

As she climbed out of the Jeep with the roses, she began to laugh. "Guess what? I just realized I've been holding these roses in my lap for a whole hour and I haven't sneezed once!" She went on to explain about her wedding bouquet. "I'm cured of my past, and you will be too, Ginger."

They followed Josh up the stone steps and through the front door into a hallway with the most beautiful marble floors which gleamed milky white below a multitiered chandelier. The sweeping staircase, with its polished dark banisters, took her breath away.

"This is like something out of the movies," she finally said.

"Come, we'll give you a tour," Josh offered.

The living room, drawing room and library all had fireplaces with elaborately carved marble mantel pieces, beautiful oil paintings hanging above them. The antique furniture and the pastel colors of the carpets and draperies spoke of quiet elegance.

One hallway on the other side of the house led to a ballroom with exquisite chandeliers. Josh flicked a switch, and the room glowed with a million points of light, delighting her.

"Belgian chandeliers," Josh said. "One of my ancestors installed them. They're a little pretentious if you ask me."

"This is awesome," Darcy said. "I'm not sure I wouldn't start acting weird if I was here for long."

"You wouldn't," he said, "because you're not trying to pretend to be somebody you're not. You're not a social climber."

He kissed her tenderly and she responded. Ginger coughed. "Listen, you two. I'm going to my room until dinner. I have to make some calls. No, Josh, don't worry, I am not calling the jail." She got teary-eyed but took a deep breath and smiled.

After she left, Josh said, "I guess she needs time alone, but I think she'll be okay. I think she's calling her friends, which is a good sign. Would you like to see my room?"

He took her up the spectacular red-carpeted stairs, holding her hand, rubbing her palm with his thumb, causing her to smile.

It was a large room, with an enormous cherry desk by the window and an old-fashioned four poster bed against one wall. It was covered with an old indigo quilt, and she imagined the pillows beneath it would be big and soft. She wanted to lie back on them and cradle his head in her own softness. She wanted his face against her bare skin.

He pulled the heavy navy blue draperies aside and pointed to the huge limbs of an oak tree that stopped short of the window by about two feet. "I'd seen too many adventure movies and wanted so badly to jump from this window to that limb. One year I tried and missed. Fortunately that other smaller branch caught my fall. I started yelling like crazy and my mother saw me from her window. You should have heard her!" Josh chuckled.

"I hope you've given up on the idea," she said, faintly alarmed that he had tried such a foolish stunt.

"Oh, yes, definitely. And it's growing thicker. In fact, I think we'll have this branch cut back. It's too inviting for kids, and we don't want—"

He wants children. The idea pleased her no end. But she was also embarrassed. He'd cut himself off, perhaps because he knew his plans did not include her. She sighed and started to walk out of the room. There was nothing new about the fact that they would go their separate ways sometime. This fabulous home only served as a reminder of their differences. Neiman Marcus versus J.C. Penney. After this weekend she would make every attempt to distance herself from him.

She stopped when she saw Ginger come to the open door. She was smiling. "I'm going over to Cindy's. Josh, can I borrow your Jeep?"

He tossed her his keys.

"Don't wait up for me," she said. "I have lots to tell them," she added sadly, over her shoulder.

Josh was still at the window, and now he pointed to where the land rose to a lush green plateau, clear of trees. "Darcy, that's where I thought Ginger's wedding would take place."

Darcy moved closer to him again; she smelled his after-shave and felt his arm come around her. "Ginger is lucky to have you, you know."

"For a while there I was beginning to think I was overreacting. Playing the protective-brother role."

She laid her head against his chest. He rested his chin on her head. His breath grazed her face, warm as an ocean breeze, and she sighed. Wordlessly he led her toward the leather couch on the other side of the room. Still standing she lifted his hand and kissed the back of it, slipping her tongue between his fingers.

He sat down on the couch and gazed at her, eyes soft, legs spread far apart.

"Come here." he said, "Closer."

She went to him willingly and stood between his knees. He took her hand in his, then clasped her to his chest, running his fingers across her back, letting his thighs press her in.

A tremor went through her, and she wrapped her arms around his shoulders. She started to tell him how much she loved him, but he was kissing her, savoring her genuine heartfelt response. He traced her collarbone with his finger, and she rearranged a lock of his hair that was falling across his forehead. He lifted the palm of her hand to his mouth and kissed it, nibbling at it.

"Let me," she whispered. Looking into the chocolate depths of his eyes, she saw a quick shimmer flash through them. *He knows I want to undress him.*

He took her hand in his and showed her he was waiting. The cold metal of his zipper under her hand brought her hot pleasure. Drawing away, she proceeded to unbutton his blue shirt, running her hands freely in the mat of rough hair on his chest.

Her lips traveled on a sensuous journey, and she heard him moan. It pleased her that he liked her touch so much. She repeated the kisses in circles around his chest, and with her thumbs she played with his tight little nipples, enjoying their stiff response. Then she left him.

Carefully she hung up his shirt on a hook by the door, titillated by his anguish for her touch. Impatiently he started to unbuckle his belt, but she stopped him. Folding his hand firmly in hers, she unhooked his pants at the waist with such keen anticipation her body shook. And then she knelt before him.

He stepped out of his pants. As he lifted a strand of hair out of her eyes, she watched, breathing hard. Such long muscular legs. So athletic. So strong. Tracing the small dark hair on his thighs with her fingertips, she sighed, enjoying the intimacy. He moaned and crumpled her hair in his fingers. She savored each touch, each kiss, reveled in the texture of his skin. And he moaned again. Her own need to press her entire body against his, to make tender love without a care in the world, escalated.

He pulled her to him and tumbled her onto the bed, then quickly did away with her clothes, flinging them to the floor. With love-softened eyes, he embraced her with a new possessiveness. And she clung to him, showering kisses on his face, welcoming his entry into her body and soul....

Sated at last, she fell asleep in his arms. He held her, carefully pulling up the white cotton sheet to cover them both.

She felt his fingers first. He picked up a lock of her hair and, kissing it, he whispered, "I love you."

She stirred and smiled and nuzzled her head on his shoulder. So this was how life was supposed to be. This was how real love could be. Then she drew herself up. "Did I just hear you say...?"

"I love you, Darcy. I have loved you for a long time now. I'm not going to let you get away again."

"I love you, too," she said. "Don't let me get away." She kissed his strong shoulders and rubbed her face on the rough patch of hair on his chest, listening to his heart thumping, feeling his breath stirring her hair.

He moaned again and lowered his head to shower kisses on her face, moving downward to flicker his loving tongue across her breasts with such tender appreciation she gasped for more.

"Gorgeous," he said between caresses.

Taking intense pleasure in his verbal and physical compliments, she eagerly welcomed him when he reached for the rest of her. Responding, texture by texture, she felt her whole heart fill with the echo of his words. *I love you.*

She wanted to hear those words again and she told him so. He complied as he held her tight and pulled her to the couch to continue expressing his love with his fingers. When he lowered his face to taste her intimately, she cried out for more. He ran his hands over the inside of her thighs, parting them, exciting new tremors that shook her even before he gave her what she wanted so desperately.

Exhausted, they lay happily crowded together on the couch. A strong sense of doing the right thing filled Darcy as much as he had, and she realized that whether it was her modest apartment or his mansion, the setting made no difference. He did.

"I'm sorry, Darcy," he said. "I was going to hire violinists, take you to a fancy restaurant, find some special way of telling you I love you."

She kissed him. "How much more special can it get?"

"I've loved you since the day I first saw you."

Shocked, she touched his face gently. "How could you have known? You didn't know me then."

"I don't know how I knew, but I knew. And when I saw you dressed as a bride, I had this wild urge to ask you to marry me on the spot. I almost did, but I got nervous."

"Really?" she said. "You cared that much for me? You know, I was really comforted by you at first, when you hugged me on that awful day. Then I thought you were hitting on me, looking for sex on the rebound, so I didn't return your calls."

"Darcy, I love you. You've given me confidence that I can make a decent family life with you. Will you marry me? I want to marry you and raise a family and get a dog like Bumpers. We can live in Washington and come out here on weekends. We could even move out here. I want to make you happy and make up for lost time. You don't have to answer this minute. I've waited so long I can wait for you to decide."

"Yes, yes, Josh, I will marry you. I love you. You've taught me to love and trust again," she whispered, then kissed him joyously.

"You're a wedding planner. Where and how would you like us to be married?"

"I want a rodeo wedding," she said simply.

He gasped. "I thought you called that dusty. You're not doing this just for me, are you?"

"Yes and no." she chuckled. "Actually I like wearing jeans and eating barbecued ribs."

The serious way he looked at her told her he knew she didn't want to wear a white wedding gown again. And he understood. He, too, wanted their day to be unique.

"Let's get married in Phoenix. We can all fly down there and have the rodeo around your grandfather's old store. We'll make it a big family event."

He laughed and hugged her, and she knew it didn't matter that he was rich and she wasn't. The wealth they shared encompassed love and trust.

After he'd dressed, he leaned across her to trace her lips with his finger. "I'll be back in a second," he said, blowing her a kiss.

She rose in a glow and began dressing. Josh fit so well into her family they would be thrilled. So would Ginger, who she loved like a sister. Josh may have been George's best man, but he truly was the better man for her.

Josh breezed back into the room and tucked her into his big warm embrace. "I love you," he said. "As I've never loved anyone or ever will. And with my grand-mother's ring, I pledge my commitment to you."

From his shirt pocket, he pulled out a ring and slipped it on her finger. She kissed him softly, knowing a circle of braided blades of grass would suit her just fine. The ring fit perfectly. He raised her hand and kissed the ring, then held up her hand to the light pouring in through the window. A round diamond, as big as a dime and set in gold, sparkled brilliant shafts of light across the room. She tilted her finger this way and that, making the light dance across his pleased face and the smile that curved her own. He watched her with tender pride, and his eyes lit up like the chandeliers downstairs. She drew him closer, letting happiness surround them.

Cowboys and babies

Roping, riding and ranching are part of cowboy life.
Diapers, pacifiers and formula are not!

At least, not until three sexy cowboys from three great
states face their greatest challenges and rewards when
confronted with a little bundle of joy.

#617 THE LAST MAN IN MONTANA (January)
#621 THE ONLY MAN IN WYOMING (February)
#625 THE NEXT MAN IN TEXAS (March)

Fan favorite Kristine Rolofson has created a wonderful
miniseries with all the appeal of the great American West
and the men and women who love the land.

Three rugged cowboys, three adorable babies—what
heroine could resist!

Available wherever Harlequin books are sold.

HARLEQUIN®

Don't miss these Harlequin favorites by some of our most distinguished authors!
And now, you can receive a discount by ordering two or more titles!

HT#25645	THREE GROOMS AND A WIFE by JoAnn Ross	$3.25 U.S. $3.75 CAN.	☐ ☐
HT#25647	NOT THIS GUY by Glenda Sanders	$3.25 U.S. $3.75 CAN.	☐ ☐
HP#11725	THE WRONG KIND OF WIFE by Roberta Leigh	$3.25 U.S. $3.75 CAN.	☐ ☐
HP#11755	TIGER EYES by Robyn Donald	$3.25 U.S. $3.75 CAN.	☐ ☐
HR#03416	A WIFE IN WAITING by Jessica Steele	$3.25 U.S. $3.75 CAN.	☐ ☐
HR#03419	KIT AND THE COWBOY by Rebecca Winters	$3.25 U.S. $3.75 CAN.	☐ ☐
HS#70622	KIM & THE COWBOY by Margot Dalton	$3.50 U.S. $3.99 CAN.	☐ ☐
HS#70642	MONDAY'S CHILD by Janice Kaiser	$3.75 U.S. $4.25 CAN.	☐ ☐
HI#22342	BABY VS. THE BAR by M.J. Rodgers	$3.50 U.S. $3.99 CAN.	☐ ☐
HI#22382	SEE ME IN YOUR DREAMS by Patricia Rosemoor	$3.75 U.S. $4.25 CAN.	☐ ☐
HAR#16538	KISSED BY THE SEA by Rebecca Flanders	$3.50 U.S. $3.99 CAN.	☐ ☐
HAR#16603	MOMMY ON BOARD by Muriel Jensen	$3.50 U.S. $3.99 CAN.	☐ ☐
HH#28885	DESERT ROGUE by Erine Yorke	$4.50 U.S. $4.99 CAN.	☐ ☐
HH#28911	THE NORMAN'S HEART by Margaret Moore	$4.50 U.S. $4.99 CAN.	☐ ☐

(limited quantities available on certain titles)

	AMOUNT	$
DEDUCT:	**10% DISCOUNT FOR 2+ BOOKS**	$
ADD:	**POSTAGE & HANDLING**	$
	($1.00 for one book, 50¢ for each additional)	
	APPLICABLE TAXES*	$_____
	TOTAL PAYABLE	$_____
	(check or money order—please do not send cash)	

To order, complete this form and send it, along with a check or money order for the total above, payable to Harlequin Books, to: **In the U.S.:** 3010 Walden Avenue, P.O. Box 9047, Buffalo, NY 14269-9047; **In Canada:** P.O. Box 613, Fort Erie, Ontario, L2A 5X3.

Name:_____

Address:_____ City:_____

State/Prov.:_____ Zip/Postal Code:_____

*New York residents remit applicable sales taxes.
  Canadian residents remit applicable GST and provincial taxes.
Look us up on-line at: http://www.romance.net

HBACK-JM4

FREE VALENTINE'S BROOCH! $9.95 U.S. retail value

This Valentine's Day Harlequin brings you all the essentials—romance, chocolate and jewelry—in:

VALENTINE *Delights*

Matchmaking chocolate-shop owner Papa Valentine dispenses sinful desserts, mouth-watering chocolates…and advice to the lovelorn, in this collection of three delightfully romantic stories by Meryl Sawyer, Kate Hoffmann and Gina Wilkins.

As our special Valentine's Day gift to you, each copy of *Valentine Delights* will have a beautiful, filigreed, heart-shaped brooch attached to the cover.

Make this your most delicious Valentine's Day ever with *Valentine Delights!*

Available in February wherever Harlequin books are sold.

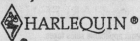

HARLEQUIN ®

Look us up on-line at: http://www.romance.net

VAL97

Heartbreak RANCH

Four generations of independent women...
Four heartwarming, romantic stories of the West...
Four incredible authors...

Fern Michaels
Jill Marie Landis
Dorsey Kelley
Chelley Kitzmiller

Saddle up with Heartbreak Ranch, an outstanding
Western collection that will take you on a whirlwind
trip through four generations and the exciting,
romantic adventures of four strong women who
have inherited the ranch from Bella Duprey,
famed Barbary Coast madam.

Available in March,
wherever Harlequin books are sold.

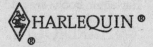

HARLEQUIN ®

Harlequin and Silhouette celebrate
Black History Month with seven terrific titles,
featuring the all-new *Fever Rising*
by Maggie Ferguson
(Harlequin Intrigue #408) and
A Family Wedding by Angela Benson
(Silhouette Special Edition #1085)!

Also available are:
Looks Are Deceiving by Maggie Ferguson
Crime of Passion by Maggie Ferguson
Adam and Eva by Sandra Kitt
Unforgivable by Joyce McGill
Blood Sympathy by Reginald Hill

On sale in January at your favorite
Harlequin and Silhouette retail outlet.